"Rick, yo

"I do now. Didn't at first but we talked a bit yesterday afternoon. Good to see you again, Cari. Hope you had a good first night home."

"It was okay," she said, the warmth of his dark blue eyes washing over her. Could it be possible that he had matured into an even better looking man than the boy she remembered? Highly possible.

Jolena's gaze shifted from Rick to Cari, her grin growing with each blink. "You two went to school together, right?"

Cari felt the crimson moving over her freckles. "Yes, we did but Rick was the big man on campus. He…we…didn't hang out together too much."

"And that's a shame," Rick replied, winking at Cari. "But high school's always hard, you know. I'm sure we've both changed since those days."

When the overly interested Jolena's eyebrows shot up, Cari slumped on her stool, wishing she could just dive under the counter. Did the man know the effect he had on women? Or did he just do this to her?

Books by Lenora Worth

Love Inspired

The Wedding Quilt
Logan's Child
I'll Be Home for Christmas
Wedding at Wildwood
His Brother's Wife
Ben's Bundle of Joy
The Reluctant Hero
One Golden Christmas
†*When Love Came to Town*
†*Something Beautiful*
†*Lacey's Retreat*
Easter Blessings
"*The Lily Field*"
‡*The Carpenter's Wife*
‡*Heart of Stone*

‡*A Tender Touch*
Blessed Bouquets
"*The Dream Man*"
A Certain Hope
A Perfect Love
A Leap of Faith
Christmas Homecoming
Mountain Sanctuary
Lone Star Secret
Gift of Wonder
The Perfect Gift
Hometown Princess

†*In the Garden*
‡*Sunset Island*
Texas Hearts

Love Inspired Suspense

Fatal Image
Secret Agent Minister
Deadly Texas Rose
A Face in the Shadows
Heart of the Night
Code of Honor

Steeple Hill

After the Storm
Echoes of Danger
Once Upon a Christmas
"*'Twas the Week*
  Before Christmas"

LENORA WORTH

has written more than forty books, most of those for Steeple Hill. She has worked freelance for a local magazine, where she wrote monthly opinion columns, feature articles and social commentaries. She also wrote for the local paper for five years. Married to her high school sweetheart for thirty-five years, Lenora lives in Louisiana and has two grown children and a cat. She loves to read, take long walks, sit in her garden and go shoe shopping.

Hometown Princess
Lenora Worth

Steeple
Hill®

Published by Steeple Hill Books™

STEEPLE HILL BOOKS

Steeple
Hill®

Recycling programs
for this product may
not exist in your area.

ISBN-13: 978-0-373-81475-6

HOMETOWN PRINCESS

Commit to the Lord whatever you do,
and your plans will succeed.
—*Proverbs* 16:3

To my sister-in-law Kathy Baker

Chapter One

It was all about the shoes.

Carinna Clark Duncan stood in front of the store window, staring at the pair of red pumps winking at her through the glass. She wanted those shoes. But she couldn't have them. Not now. Maybe not ever. Her days of extravagant shoe shopping were over. *Lead me not to temptation, Lord.*

She glanced around the quaint main street of Knotwood Mountain, Georgia, and then looked to her left at the old run-down turn-of-the-century Victorian house she'd inherited after her father's death a month ago. Duncan House—that's what her parents had called it. Now it had a dilapidated old sign that said Photography and Frames—Reasonable Prices hanging off one of the porch beams. Her childhood home had been reduced to a business rental, but the last renter had left in a hurry from what she'd been told by her father's lawyer.

The house was the only part of James Duncan's vast estate she'd received. The bitterness and pain rose up like bile inside her. But it wasn't because she wanted the whole estate, even though some cold hard cash would be good right now. No, her deep-seated resentment and anger came from another source. And her prayers for release hadn't worked.

This anger and jealousy was toward the woman who'd swooped in and wooed Cari's still-grieving father into marrying her just months after Cari's mother had died. That woman, Doreen Stillman, and her two children, had managed not only to fool Cari's vulnerable father for the last few years; they'd also managed to turn him against his only daughter. The daughter who'd loved and adored him and still grieved for her mother and him so much it woke her up in tears in the middle of the night.

Once the apple of her doting father's eye, Cari had soon become the outcast, the troublemaker who stood against Doreen. And

Doreen made sure James Duncan knew this, made sure he heard all about how horribly Cari treated Doreen and her children. Even if it wasn't true, even if she'd been the one who'd been mistreated, there was no way to convince her besotted, grief-stricken father. No way. And now it was too late to make amends with him. Cari only hoped she'd been able to get through to him enough before he died to make him understand that she loved him.

Staring at the shoes with a Monday morning moroseness, she thought it was pretty ironic that a pair of shoes had started the whole chain of events that had eventually caused Cari to fall out of her father's good graces in the first place. Cari and her younger stepsister Bridget had been fighting over a pair of blue sandals. They belonged to Cari, but Bridget had insisted she wanted to borrow them. Cari had refused, saying Bridget was too young and her feet too long for the narrow, strappy shoes that Cari intended to wear to a party that night. But Doreen and Cari's father had sided with Bridget. Cari had not only lost the shoes— Bridget never gave them back—she'd also lost a lot of respect for her father. And apparently, he'd lost respect for her, too. Things had gone from bad to worse after that. Her once storybook life had become miserable.

But he had left her the house.

That alone had sustained Cari after his death. He'd left her the one thing she remembered with happiness and joy—the house where she'd grown up with both her parents. It had been a loving, wonderful, faith-filled home back then, full of adventure and all the things a little girl loved, including a turret room. Cari used to pretend she was a princess; she'd dreamed big dreams in that round little room just off her bedroom on the right side of the two-story house. Now, the pretty memories faded and she was left staring at a harsh reality.

Doreen had immediately moved the family out to a big, modern house on the Chattahoochee River and convinced James to let the town rezone this house for commercial use. Only she'd neglected to take care of this particular piece of property. Doreen wouldn't know a house with good bones if it fell on her.

The old house was still solid, but it needed a lot of cosmetic work, Cari thought. And so did she. Maybe she could make some sense of things, redoing this old place. Maybe. By leaving her the house, her father had given her a new lease on life. She once again had big dreams—for herself and for the house she had opened up earlier today. She planned to renovate it room by room. And she planned to open a quaint little boutique to showcase her jewelry and trinkets on the first floor. She could live on the second floor. It would be a great arrangement if she could make a go of it. *Please, God, let me do this right.*

But she did have another big problem. A definite lack of capital. She had to figure out a way to find the money to do everything she envisioned. From the research she'd done, a loan didn't look possible.

She turned back to the shoes, a longing bursting through her heart. She was a material girl—or at least she used to be. She reminded herself that those days were gone and so she couldn't afford the shoes. But she sure did admire them anyway.

Just keep on admiring, she told herself. And remember why you're here. You have something else to focus on now besides shopping. You have a home.

Cari thanked God and thanked her father.

Maybe this was his way of telling her he had loved her in spite of everything. And she knew in her heart God had never abandoned her, even if it had felt that way since she'd become an exile from Knotwood Mountain.

The sound of shifting gears caused her to turn around. The bright summer sun shone brightly on the battered old brown-and-white open Jeep pulling up to the curb. The man driving downshifted and cut the roaring engine then hopped out, heading toward where Cari stood in front of Adams General Store and Apparel.

"Go on in and try them on," he said with a grin, motioning toward the shoes.

And Cari turned and faced another dream she'd forgotten. Rick Adams. In the flesh and looking too bright and way too good with the early-morning sunlight glinting across his auburn-brown curly hair. Did he remember her? Cari doubted it. He'd been a few years older and he'd run with a different crowd in high school. The fun football and cheerleader crowd. While she'd preferred reading sappy fiction on most Saturday nights and observing him from afar on most school days. The classic tale of the plain Jane wanting the handsome prince, with no happy ending in sight.

"Hi," she said with a stiff smile. "I can't try them on. I can't afford them." Honesty was her new policy.

He gave her a blue-eyed appraisal but she didn't see recognition in that enticing stare. "Too bad. I think they'd fit you just right."

She shook her head. "I don't think so. And don't tempt me. I've got to get going." She didn't give him time to talk her into trying on the gorgeous shoes. Cari hurried to the rambling house next door and quickly went inside.

"Did you see Cari out there?"

Rick looked up at his mother's words, spoken from the second floor of Adams General Store and Apparel. Gayle was leaning over the timbered banister holding an armful of women's T-shirts with the words *I rode the river at Knotwood Mountain* emblazed across them, grinning down at her son.

"Cari? Cari who?"

"Cari Duncan. I thought I saw you talking to her."

Rick glanced outside then back up at his mom. "That pretty strawberry-blonde looking at the red shoes in the window? That was shy little Cari Duncan?"

"That's her—back home and about to open up her own shop right next door in the old Duncan House, according to Jolena." Gayle put the shirts on a nearby rack and came down the stairs. "Jolena told me all about it when I went by the diner this morning."

Rick looked up at his mother, his hands on his hips. "Why didn't I know about this?"

Gayle let out a chuckle. "Maybe because you missed the chamber of commerce meeting last night—again. Everyone was talking about it, Jolena said. And apparently, Doreen was fit to be tied because she planned to sell the house and turn a tidy profit on that corner lot."

Rick groaned. "I completely forgot the meeting. I had to get all this fishing gear and our rafts and floats ready for the summer crowds." He couldn't believe he'd just talked to Cari and hadn't even realized it was her. "Well, I'm glad someone's taking over the old place. It's an eyesore and last time I did attend a meeting, everyone on First Street agreed something needed to be done about it."

Gayle busied herself with straightening the bait-and-tackle rack by the cash register. "Doreen didn't worry about the upkeep on the place. I'm sure she's unhappy that it no longer belongs to her." She pursed her lips. "You know, that's all Cari got from the inheritance."

"You're kidding?" Rick went back to the window. "Her father owned half the property in town and she got stuck with that old house. That building needs to be overhauled. It's gone to ruin since the last tenant left."

"Doreen kicked the last tenant out," Gayle replied as she poured him a cup of coffee off the stove at the back of the store. "She's not an easy landlady from what I've heard."

"Then she probably wasn't an easy step-mother either," Rick countered. "I hope Cari can stand up to the woman. She was always so passive and shy in high school." Not that he hadn't noticed her pretty turquoise eyes and nice smile back then. But that was about as far as Rick had ever gotten with Cari. His girlfriend hadn't liked him being kind to a girl she considered "a boring little spoiled princess."

The girlfriend was long gone, and well… Cari was back and right next door, and she didn't look boring at all. The hometown princess was all grown-up. He'd have to go and visit her, apologize for not recognizing her.

"I can't believe I didn't know it was her," he said to his mother. "She's changed."

"Yes, lost weight and cut her hair. She's downright spunky-looking now," Gayle said as she grabbed one of Jolena's famous cinnamon rolls and headed back up to the women's department of the sprawling store. "And she'll need to be spunky if she intends to renovate that place. We'll have to offer her some help. Be neighborly."

Rick grinned then headed to the stockroom. He'd have to be neighborly another day. He had lots to do today. Only a few weeks until the Fourth of July and the flood of tourists who'd come to Knotwood Mountain to camp, fish, swim and go tubing and rafting on the nearby Chattahoochee River. And hopefully shop at Adams General Store and Apparel for all their outfitter needs.

They'd made this store a nice place since he'd come back five years ago. His mother had taken over the top floor for her women's apparel, knickknacks, souvenirs and artwork and he had the bottom floor for more manly stuff like rafting and fishing gear, rugged outdoor clothes and shoes and cowboy and work boots. And since his older brother Simon designed handmade cowboy boots in a studio just outside of town on their small ranch, Rick also had the pleasure of selling his brother's popular boots both retail and online. A nice setup and, finally, one that was seeing a profit. He wished his father was still alive to see how he'd turned the old family store into a tourist attraction.

But…wishes didn't get the work done, so he went into the stockroom and headed to the back alley, intent on unloading and inventorying stock in between customers for the rest of the day.

First, he had to gather the empty boxes from yesterday and take them out to the recycling bin before the truck came cruising through. Always something to do around this place, that was for sure. But Rick liked the nice steady work and the casual atmosphere. It sure beat his hectic, stressful lifestyle back in Atlanta.

He'd put all of that behind him now. He'd come home.

He stopped at the trash dump and stared at the leaning back porch of Cari's place, wondering what had brought her back. Surely not just this old Victorian diamond in the rough.

He was about to turn and head back inside

when the door of the house creaked open and he heard a feminine voice shouting, "Shoo, get out of here."

Out swooped a pigeon, flapping its wings as it lifted into the air.

The woman stood on the porch with her hands on her hips, smiling up at the terrified bird. "And don't come back. I'm the only squatter allowed on these premises now."

Rick let out a hoot of laughter. "Poor little pigeon."

Cari whirled, mortified that Rick had heard her fussing at the innocent pigeon. "Oh, hi. Sorry but it was either him or me. He's made a mess of what used to be a storage room, I think. And I'm pretty sure he's had a few feathered friends over for some wild parties, too. First thing on my list—fix that broken windowpane."

Rick strolled over toward the porch then looked up at her. "Cari," he said, his smile sharp enough to burn away all the cobwebs she had yet to clear out of the first floor. "You've changed."

Cari pushed at her shaggy, damp hair. This pleasant morning was fast turning into a hot afternoon. "Same old me," she said, wondering if he was even taller now. "I figured you didn't recognize me, though." And he'd aged to perfection, curly brown hair, crinkling, laughing eyes.

"No, sorry I didn't. But it's sure nice to see you again. It's been a while."

She leaned on the rickety old railing, the sound of the river gurgling over the nearby rocks soothing her frazzled mind. "Yep. Last time I saw you, you were off to Georgia Tech with a cheerleader on your arm. How'd that go for you?"

He shook his head, looked down at his work boots. "Not too well at first. I partied more than I studied and the cheerleader found her one true love—it wasn't me. Just about flunked out. My old man didn't appreciate my lack of commitment, let me tell you. But I finally got things together and pulled through."

Cari nodded, noting the darkening in his eyes when he mentioned his father. "I did the same thing—didn't party too much, just didn't much care. I did flunk out at the University of Georgia. But I eventually went back and studied design and got a major in business. Little good that did me, however." She didn't want to elaborate and she hoped he wouldn't ask her to.

He didn't. Instead he looked off into the ridge of mountains to the west. "But here you are, about to open a business right here in Knotwood Mountain." He moved a little closer, one booted foot on the battered steps. "What's the plan, anyway?"

Cari eyed the old porch and the broken steps. "The plan is to get this house back the way I remember it." Except it wouldn't be the same. Nothing would ever be the same. "Why is it when a house is shut down it seems to wither and die?"

Rick lifted his gaze to the dormer windows and the gabled roof. "I guess because houses are a lot like people. They need to be needed."

Surprised that he'd turned all mushy about things, she decided to stick to a safer conversation. "I've got my things stored in Atlanta but I'm bringing them here in a few days. All the inventory left over from the shop I had there. And I want to order lots of other things. It'll take a while to get it going, but I think with the tourist traffic I might be able to make it work. I checked around and Knotwood Mountain doesn't have a shabby-chic boutique."

He squinted up at her. "That's a mighty big plan."

"Yes, it is. And I have a mighty tiny budget."

"You been to the bank for a loan?"

"Working on it." She wondered if the local banker would even talk to her. Doreen carried a lot of weight in town. But the Duncan name still stood for something. At least Cari had that. That and about two nickels to rub together.

Rick looked up and down the alley then back up at her. "Well, maybe it'll work out for you. What about your business? What kind of establishment will this be? And what exactly is shabby-chic?"

That was a subject she could talk about for hours. "I design jewelry. I take old estate jewelry and rework it then resell it. I also carry unique women's clothing and I fix up picture frames and jewelry boxes, trinkets— I like to take old things and make them pretty again. Sometimes I redesign tote bags and purses."

"Purses?" He grinned up at her again. "Maybe you can make one to go with those red shoes in my window."

"I told you, I can't afford those shoes."

He pushed off the steps. "Nobody can. My mother ordered them at market on an impulse and now they're just sitting there waiting for the right feet—and the right amount of money. Maybe those pumps have been waiting for you. And something tells me you'll work hard until you *can* afford them."

Cari's heart soared. It had been a while since anyone had expressed belief in her. A very long time. "You think so?"

He tipped a finger to his temple in salute. "If you can take on this old house then I'd say you can do anything." Then he smiled and walked back toward the open double doors of the general store's stockroom. But he turned and gave her a long, studied look. "Good to have you back. And if you need anything, anything at all, you call me, okay, Princess?"

"Thanks." Cari watched him go back inside then looked up at the mountain vista just beyond town. The Blue Ridge Mountains had always brought her peace. Even while she'd lived in Athens and later in Atlanta, she'd often come up here to the mountains just to get away. Of course, she'd never come back here to Knotwood Mountain, but there were other spots nearby she loved, where the rhododendrons bloomed in bright whites and pinks and grew six feet tall. She stood listening and silent, the sound of the river gurgling through the middle of town continuing to bring her a sense of peace and comfort.

"Can I do this, Lord?" she asked. Had she made the right decision, leaving Atlanta to come home? What choice did she have? she wondered.

After all, this old house was all she had now.

She'd pretty much wasted away her bank account and she'd maxed out her charge cards. All in the name of looking good, looking up-to-date and in style while trying to keep up with a man who never intended to settle down and marry her. All in the name of a facade that could never quite fill the void inside her heart.

Turning to head back inside, she thought about the red shoes and all they represented. Once, she would have marched inside the store and bought them without giving it a second thought. Just to make herself feel better.

Looking over at the general store, she whispered, "Sorry, Rick, but I'm not a princess anymore."

Once, when she'd been frivolous and im-pulsive and careless, she would have spent money she didn't have. But that Cari was gone, just like the passive, shy Cari from high school. This new, more assertive Cari was going to have to reinvent herself, one step at a time and on her own two feet.

Only this time, she wouldn't be wearing fabulous shoes or be hiding behind a carefully controlled facade when she did it.

Chapter Two

The next morning, Cari opened the door to Jolena's Diner and smiled at her friend. "Hello."

"Well, look what the cat dragged in," Jolena, big, black and beautiful, said with a white, toothy grin, reaching to give Cari a tight hug. "How was your first day home, suga'?"

Cari sat down on one of the bright red stools at the long white counter. "Different." She'd managed to get the kitchen clean enough to boil water and make toast and she'd slept on an air mattress in a small room upstairs. "I cleaned all day and unpacked enough clothes and essentials to get me through for a while. I'm going to pick up a few groceries and toiletry items. And I'm praying the bathroom upstairs will stay in working order until I can have a plumber check the whole place."

Jolena looked doubtful. "You could have stayed with us, you know."

Cari took the coffee Jolena automatically handed her, the hustle and bustle of this bright, popular diner making her feel alive. The smell of bacon and eggs reminded her she hadn't eaten much since early yesterday. The buzz of conversation reminded her how lonely and isolated she'd become in the past few weeks. But Jolena's smile held Cari together.

"I appreciate the offer, but I didn't want to put your girls out of their bedrooms."

Jolena grunted. "Those four—honey, they're always in each other's way so one more wouldn't even be noticed. Even a cute one with freckles like you."

"I did just fine on my own last night," Cari said. Never mind that she hadn't actually slept very much. But the moonlight coming through the old sheers in the room had given her a sense of security at least. "I have a bed and I scrubbed the kitchen and the storage room yesterday. Of course, I need a new stove and a refrigerator. That ice chest isn't going to work in this summer heat."

Jolena nodded. "I can hook you up with my friend down at the appliance store. He'll make you a deal."

Cari laughed at the woman who'd been friends with her mother, Natalie, since they were both little girls. Finding pen and paper, she wrote down the name and number. "You always have connections."

Jolena let out a belly laugh then waved to two departing fishermen. "Yes, I sure do. And speaking of that—you need a makeover, honey. You look a little peaked."

Cari pushed at her hair. "I guess I do look bad, but I wasn't too concerned with my appearance this morning. I don't have any groceries yet and I just needed coffee, badly."

"And so do I," said a masculine voice behind her.

Cari pivoted so fast she almost fell off her perch. "Rick, good morning." Pushing at her hair again, she wished she'd at least bothered to put on lipstick.

Jolena leaned over the counter, her long thin braids tapping her robust shoulders. "Rick, you remember our Cari, don't you?"

Rick sat down next to Cari and took the cup of coffee a waitress brought him. "I do now. Didn't at first but we talked a bit yesterday

afternoon. Good to see you again, Cari. Hope
you had a good first night home."

"It was okay," she said, the warmth of his
dark blue eyes washing over her. Could it be
possible that he had matured into an even
better looking man than the boy she remembered? Highly possible.

Jolena's gaze shifted from Rick to Cari,
her grin growing with each blink. "You two
went to school together, right?"

Cari felt the crimson moving over her
freckles. "Yes, we did but Rick was the big
man on campus. He…we…didn't hang out
together too much."

"And that's a shame," Rick replied, winking at Cari. "But high school's always hard,
you know. I'm sure we've both changed
since those days."

When Jolena's overly interested eyebrows
shot up, Cari slumped on her stool, wishing
she could just dive under the counter. Did the
man know the effect he had on women? Or
did he just do this to her? She felt all mushy
and soft-kneed. Which was just plain crazy.
She wasn't in high school anymore. And she
had changed. She didn't trust pretty boys
anymore and she sure didn't indulge in ado-
lescent crushes these days.

Finally, because he was still smiling at her, she said, "So why'd you come back to Knotwood Mountain, Rick?"

The smile softened and his rich blue eyes went black. "That's a long story and, unfortunately, I don't have time to tell it right now. I've got people waiting to rent tubes for the day." He got up, took his to-go cup of coffee and lifted it toward Jolena. "Put it on my tab." Then he turned to Cari. "I'll see you around, neighbor."

Cari waited until she heard the screen door slap back on its hinges then looked at Jolena. "What? Did I ask the wrong question?"

Jolena, known as much for her gossip as her soul food, leaned close, her dimples deepening. "I heard it had something to do with a bad breakup. I think the man was heartbroken and hurting when he came limping into town. But he's good now, real good. And *real* available."

Cari almost spit out her sip of coffee. "Yes, so available that he practically ran out of here. If he can't talk about her, then he ain't over her."

"He might get over her better if he had someone sweet to talk to, know what I mean?"

"I do know what you mean, but I'm not here to find a man, Jolena. Just like Rick there, I, too, went through a bad breakup—with the man and with my money that the man took." She pointed across the street. "You see that wilted wedding cake of a house sitting over there. I'm here to fix that house up and get my boutique going. That's about all I have any time or energy for. And I don't want a man standing around telling me what to do and making me feel guilty about everything from the shoes I wear to the friends I have. I want to do this my way."

Jolena wasn't to be hushed. "You got a point there, honey. But you need to take time to be friendly to the other merchants along the street. We stick together around here. You'll see. Don't be all mean and standoffish with Rick Adams. You might need a friend, too. But that attitude will surely scare people away."

Cari couldn't deny that she needed to make a connection. But with Rick? Friend and neighboring merchant, maybe. But that would have to be it. Still, it wouldn't hurt to know more about him—just so she'd know what *not* to ask him next time she saw him.

"Okay, so he is good-looking," she

admitted on a low whisper. "It won't be very hard to be nice to him. But that's as far as it goes."

Jolena made an exaggerated frown. "Girl, that man is so pretty, well, as my mama used to say, you could spoon him up like sugar."

Cari had to laugh. "Your mama would tell you to put your big brown eyes right back inside your head, too, if she were here—since you're married and have four children."

"You are so right," Jolena said, waving a glitter-nailed finger in Cari's face. "But what's your excuse, honey? Beside thinking all men are the scum of the earth, I mean?"

Cari frowned right back at her friend. "Me? I am not the least bit interested, especially in someone like Rick Adams. From what I remember back in high school, he had a new girl on his arm every Friday night."

"This ain't high school, girl, and you've changed since then. Maybe he has, too. He said as much himself." Jolena fluffed her heavy reddish-brown weave, her words echoing Cari's own earlier thoughts. "His mother is a good Christian woman, you know. Gives to the local food bank and works there, too. Helps out with the youth at church just about every Sunday night. And my mama says Rick has settled down, changed his wild ways since his father passed."

That caught Cari's attention. Had Rick had father issues just like her? "Tell me more," she said, smiling over at Jolena. "And while you're at it, can I have a short-stack with fresh strawberries?"

Jolena was more than happy to oblige.

Rick Adams. The second son of the late Lazaro Adams and widow Gayle Miller Adams. After her husband's death, Gayle Adams had turned her husband's Western and outfitter store into a haven for artists and craftsmen, including herself and her oldest son Simon. Then she'd put in a women's clothing department on the second floor. According to Jolena, the big old store had struggled after Mr. Adams had died, but now her good-looking second son was back from the big city and working hard in the family business.

Wonder what the whole story there is, Cari mused as she waited for Jolena to ring up a customer. She knew why she'd come home, but Rick? Could a woman have messed him up that badly? From what she'd heard from Jolena, he'd had it made in Atlanta. Big-time marketing guru, all-around business tycoon, etc. While she'd been mostly miserable and alienated from her father, and definitely messed up from too many bad relationships. But maybe being successful didn't help in the love department. It sure hadn't helped ease her misery and unhappiness.

"So that's supposed to make me sit up and take notice?" Cari asked when Jolena came back. "Just because he's successful in business does not mean he's ready for a relationship, especially if he's been burned before. And we can't know if he's changed from high school. Some people change, some people don't."

"You gotta have faith, honey," Jolena said, rolling her eyes. "Haven't I told you, if you turn it over to the Lord—"

"The Lord will turn it all to good," Cari finished, her voice low so she wouldn't attract attention. "Well, you know how I feel about that. The Lord hasn't provided me with the answers I need lately. Not since the day Doreen Stillman and her two spoiled children walked into my father's house."

Jolena's dark face turned serious and somber as the conversation shifted to the subject Cari couldn't get off her mind. "Cari, honey, it's been over eight years and your father has left this earth. You need to make peace with what happened. And with what *didn't* happen."

Cari shook her head, causing sprigs of curling strawberry-blond hair to fall around her face. "I can't do that, Jolena. I barely got to visit him when he was ill, and that's because of Doreen's hovering over him. He never once told me he'd forgiven me. And I prayed for that every day. I tried to tell him that I loved him, but I think it was too late. He was too sick to understand."

"I know things were rough," Jolena said, her sequined mauve sundress flashing with each wave of her hand. "Prayer is good but wanting to get back at your stepmother even after the man is dead and gone is not so good. Eight years is a long time to hold that kind of grudge, honey."

"The woman used my father."

"You think. You haven't seen anything to indicate that and she did stick around for all those years you were gone, remember?"

Cari cringed but held firm. "I lived with them before he kicked me out. I saw her in action. She married him for one reason. She wanted his money. And now, she has it."

Jolena twirled a plump dark ringlet. "She

might have his estate, but if what you say is true that woman will pay her dues one day, mark my words. I just don't want you to be the one who gets hurt all over again trying to see that she does."

"I understand," Cari said, the words a low growl, her fork stuck to a fluffy chunk of pancake. "But my mother had only been dead three months when Doreen moved in on my still-grieving father. I became a stranger in my own home, and she somehow alienated my father from me to the point that he practically threw me out on the street. I left before that happened but things sure went downhill from there."

Jolena's dark eyes filled with understanding. "So you made a few mistakes, did some things you're not proud of. We've all been there, suga'. But look at you now."

"Yes, look at me," Cari replied, her voice shaking in spite of her stiff-necked pride. "I don't exist anymore, Jolena. I didn't exist to my father and we lost precious time. Now I have to do something to honor him. Renovating this house will do that. And give me something solid to focus on, at least."

Jolena grabbed Cari's hand and held it in hers. "I understand you're in pain, you're hurting, baby. But I promised your dear mother that I would watch over you. I can't do that if you keep insisting on giving me the slip and going off to do foolish things."

"You mean, like trying to confront Doreen?"

"Exactly," Jolena said through a sigh. "I like it better when you're positive and purposeful. You know the Lord wants you to have a purpose."

Cari laughed at that. "A purpose is one thing, but not having the funds to make purposeful things happen is another."

"Are you going to the bank?"

"Yes, in a couple of days. I have to get everything together and ply my case."

Jolena put her hands underneath her chin and smiled over at Cari. "Eat your pancakes and let me do the worrying. You want that old house to shine? Well, you can't do that all on your own. Just let Jolena here do some thinking. I might have an idea to help you out."

Cari was afraid to ask what that idea was, but knowing Jolena, it would be big and bold. And it would probably involve a certain handsome businessman, too. Jolena never tired of matchmaking and being bossy for a good cause.

Could she allow that to happen? Could she become a true part of the town she'd fled all those years ago? Could she ask for help, knowing that Doreen now held the upper hand? If Cari wanted her business to work, she'd have to learn to be more decisive and assertive instead of hanging back in the shadows. That would be the only sure way to get even with Doreen, to prove the woman wrong. She'd have to work at getting to know people she'd long ago forgotten. And that might mean being civil to a woman she detested. And becoming close to a man she'd never really forgotten. Fat chance of anything other than friendship with Rick Adams, however.

She needed to find the strength to stand on her own two feet, once and for all. Self-control and fortitude—that was what she needed now. And if that meant being nice to her neighbors, including Doreen Duncan, and working for the good of this beautiful little village, then she could do that, too. Her father had left her this house for a reason. It was time Cari tried to figure out that reason.

She'd play nice with the community leaders and she'd work hard to make a go of her business. She knew how to do that, at least.

And one day maybe she could finally be proud and self-assured enough to accept that in his own stubborn way her father might have loved her and believed in her after all.

Chapter Three

Armed with a cheeseburger for lunch, Cari headed back to the house to get busy. She had to call the contractor she'd hired and find out when he could start the renovations, that is, if he could give her a good quote. Then she wanted to call the phone company to get a landline for the boutique. Eventually, she'd need a computer for both the cash register and for placing orders. She'd also need to rebuild her Web site with the new location. But for now, her old laptop would have to do for some of that.

If she could get the bottom floor repaired and updated over the next few weeks and generate some revenue, she'd worry about the upstairs later. She'd read up on renovating old homes and all the advice said to take it one room at a time, starting with the most urgent ones. Maybe she could save some money by starting the preliminary work herself and leave the hard stuff to the contractor.

Doreen had left several pieces of antique furniture scattered throughout the house. The woman didn't know a thing about high-quality furniture but that would work to Cari's advantage now. She'd dusted and polished the old Queen Anne buffet she'd found in the parlor. That would make a nice display table and she could use the drawers to store jewelry and small items such as scarves and belts.

There was an old four-poster oak bed upstairs. It was rickety and needed some tender loving care, but it would be a jewel when Cari refinished it. She'd put it in the turret room and make it her own. With the few other pieces she'd found, she had enough to do some sparse decorating.

"Well, I'd say the kitchen and bathroom down here are both really urgent." But they were both clean now and she had the callused, rough hands to prove it. The bathroom was in fairly good working order, but it needed new fixtures and, well, new everything.

She put the cheeseburger bag on the now clean but chipped linoleum counter then turned to admire her handiwork in the old kitchen. The rickety white table and chairs had been scrubbed and looked halfway decent, but the old cabinets needed to be completely redone. They were high and big with plenty of good storage space. That was a plus. She'd gone through them and wiped them down then placed shelf liners in each one. She had a few mismatched dishes she'd unpacked and her coffeepot. Fresh daisies in a Mason jar made the old white table seem almost happy.

Some groceries would help. And a refrigerator. Standing in the long wide kitchen, she called the man Jolena had suggested. He immediately gave her some quotes on various sizes and styles. Cari thanked him and told him she'd be out to look this afternoon. Having taken care of that, she surveyed the kitchen again, memories washing over her with a gentleness that reminded her of her mother.

The room was long and wide and filled with windows that had once looked out over a vast backyard that ran all the way down to the nearby river. That backyard had been sold in increments as First Street commercialism had continued to grow right into the old suburban Victorian neighborhood built along the Chattahoochee River.

Duncan House was one of the few remaining original homes built here at the turn of the century. Most of them has been razed or renovated beyond recognition to make way for progress. And while Cari was thankful that her small town was now a tourist mecca, she sure wanted to bring back some of that Victorian charm that had once colored the place.

"Starting with Duncan House."

Maybe she'd update the kitchen to make it functional for events and turn it into a nice sitting area for customers. She could bring over some cookies and pies from Jolena's Diner and serve them with coffee and tea from the old antique sideboard shoved up against one wall. Just like her mother used to do when they'd invited company over for Sunday dinner.

"And where will I get the money for that?" she wondered, thinking she only had a few thousand in her bank account and her one remaining charge card was for emergencies only. Getting a bank loan scared her silly since her credit history wasn't the best, but she had to try.

Determination and the financial budget she'd worked so hard to create and maintain over the past couple of years driving her on, Cari put away her bag and decided, now that she'd cleared and cleaned the downstairs open area, she'd give the bathroom one more thorough cleaning. She could then tackle the upstairs again, just to make sure she hadn't missed anything.

First on the list would be to make sure the stairs were safe. They'd seemed a bit wobbly yesterday when she'd ventured up to see her turret room. That was another thing on the list—the turret room was intact but dirty and waterlogged from broken windowpanes. The pigeons seemed to love to roost there, too.

"Too bad about that."

She remembered the room when it had been all bright whites and feminine blues and yellows, with a tiny little table and chairs and a real porcelain tea set where she'd entertained her dolls and, sometimes, her father and mother, too. Cari had clopped around in a big hat and a pair of feather-encrusted plastic high heels, a princess content in her own skin. And very innocent and naive in her security.

"Too bad about that, too."

But she intended to restore the room in those same sky-blues and sunshine-yellows, using a hydrangea theme since the old bushes out front were still intact and blooming to beat the band.

Hearing the front door squeak open, she wondered if the contractor was here already.

"Ye-hoo? Anybody home?"

Doreen. Cari gave herself a mental shake. She wouldn't let that woman get to her. Taking a deep, calming breath, she called out, "I'm in the kitchen."

Doreen came through the arched doorway to stop just inside the empty kitchen, her gaze sweeping the room with distaste. "I just had to come and see for myself if all the rumors I kept hearing were true." Patting her bright red teased hair, she shook her head and rolled her eyes. "You can't be serious, Cari."

Cari prayed for patience. Putting her hands down beside her jeans so she wouldn't use them to do physical harm, she lifted her eyebrows. "Serious? Oh, you mean about reopening Duncan House? Yes, I'm very serious."

Doreen dropped her designer bag on the table. "I heard about it at the chamber of commerce meeting the other night and I just couldn't believe my ears. I mean, I knew your father left this old place to you—why, I'll never understand. But honestly, I expected you to call me, begging me to list it, just to get it off your hands."

Cari couldn't believe the audacity of this vile woman. "Why would I do that, Doreen? This is all I have left. You managed to get the rest."

Score one for Cari. The woman bristled to the point of turning as red as her dyed hair. "Your father left everything to me because he knew you'd just squander it away. I mean, c'mon, now, Cari, you don't actually think you can make a go of things in this old building, do you? The last tenant found out pretty quick that this place is way too far gone to run a business in. The utilities alone are over the top."

"From what I heard, you charged the last tenant too much rent and made too many demands for him to keep his photography and frame business going. I heard he moved to a new strip mall out on I-75 and he's doing great."

"That obnoxious man—I was glad to be rid of him. Always calling wanting something fixed, something changed. Impossible to deal with."

Doreen wouldn't give an inch, Cari knew. So she didn't try to argue with the woman. "I'm here to stay, Doreen. Get used to it."

Doreen grabbed her purse. "We'll see how long you last. You know, if you get desperate and want to sell, I'll cut you a deal. I'd planned to have this place torn down and if we both play our cards right, that can still happen. I'll be glad to take it off your hands and for a fair price, too."

"Why would you want to do that?" Cari asked. "Especially since you didn't take care of it when you were the landlord?"

"I had other priorities," Doreen shot back, the crow's feet around her eyes lined with too much concealer. "But now that your father is gone, well, I'm being a bit more aggressive in buying up more property." She swept the room with a harsh glance. "This should have stayed mine anyway. But I'm willing to buy it back and then maybe you can get out from under that mound of debt you brought back with you. If you change your mind, you know where to find me."

"I won't," Cari said, seething underneath her calm. Buy it back? Over her dead body.

She waited until the annoying clicking sound of Doreen's pumps had left the building then turned and ran out the back door to catch her breath. Leaning over the old railing, Cari felt sick to her stomach. Feeling tears of frustration she didn't dare shed, she held her head down and stared at an efficient ant trail moving steadily along the crack in the steps.

"We have to stop meeting like this."

She looked up to find Rick standing there staring at her, his smile friendly, his eyes calm.

Cari inhaled a deep breath. "You mean out in the alley, while I'm having a hissy fit?"

"Is that what you're having? I would have never guessed." Even though he was smiling, she appreciated the concern in his eyes.

Cari shook her hair off her face. "The wicked stepmother just paid me a friendly visit. Offered to buy me out. Can you believe that after the way she let this place get all run-down?"

Rick could tell she was hanging on by a thread, so he decided to keep things light. "Interesting that she'd even suggest that. I saw her taking off on her broom a couple of minutes ago so you're safe for now. If it's any consolation, she looked madder than a wet hornet."

"That does make me feel better," Cari replied, her eyes brightening. "I shouldn't let her get to me, but she does. She always has."

He sat down on the steps. "Got a minute to chat?"

She looked back inside. "Sure, none of this is going anywhere soon. And if I don't get a bank loan, it's not going to change anytime soon."

Rick understood she had a lot on her mind, but he needed to clarify something. "Look, Cari, about earlier at the diner when you asked me why I came back here?"

She put a hand over her eyes. "Oh, you mean when I was being completely nosy and out of line?"

"You weren't out of line. Nosy, yes, but out of line, no. It's just that I don't like to talk about my reasons for coming home. It's… complicated."

She slapped him on the arm. "Tell me something I don't know. I'm the queen of complicated homecomings."

His expression relaxed as he let out a long sigh. "Seems we both came back here to prove something to somebody, maybe?"

"Now who's being nosy?"

"Okay, I admit I'm wondering why you did come back and especially to such a challenging project?"

She put her head in her hands and stared down at her pink toenails. "My father left me this house. After our rocky relationship, that was enough reason for me."

Rick knew right then and there that Cari Duncan was someone special. And he could certainly understand the concept of needing something to hold on to, some sort of validation from a loved one. "Well, my father left the general store to my mother and my brother and me and one of the reasons I came home was to make sure we kept the legacy of his hard work alive and thriving. My brother Simon is an introverted artist, a boot maker who lost his wife a few years back. He didn't want anything to do with running a retail store and, honestly, he doesn't have time. And my mom tried her best to keep things going but she was working herself into an early grave, just like my dad. I had to come home to help. And…I needed to get away from Atlanta. You know, that same old crowd—hard to shake."

She didn't respond at first. She just sat

looking at her feet. Then she said, "Funny, I loved the crowds. I lived in Athens after college and then moved to Atlanta. I had a good job—a career, with my own boutique and employees who worked hard selling my designs and other brands. I was in an upscale part of town and I was making pretty good money. I partied and laughed and played and spent way too much money trying to keep up with the crowd, trying to live up to this image I had of myself. It caught up with me when I fell for the wrong man. He decided he liked my cash flow a lot more than he loved me. I carried him after he lost his job—bad idea. I went into debt trying to buy his love. But I got rid of the slacker boyfriend and I got help from this very strict financial advisor who put me on a tough budget. I've managed to pay off a lot of it and I've even saved a little bit—a first for me."

"So you came home to start over."

She looked up finally, her eyes glistening like muted turquoise glass. "Yes, and to fix the mistakes I made with my father. Only, it's too late, I think."

Rick looked around at the pines and oaks out beyond the honeysuckle vines lining the alley wall. A cool breeze moved over the oak trees and played through the wind chimes his mother had hung at the back door of the general store. "I'm sorry you lost your father, but if he left you this place then it has to mean something, right?"

"That's what I'm hoping," she said. "And that's what I want to figure out. Why did he leave me this house when he seemed so distant in life? Is that too weird?"

The little catch of doubt in her words held him. "Not weird at all. I think it's rather noble to want to fix this place up, to honor your parents."

"But foolish?"

"Nope. Just as long as you don't let she-who-won't-be-named get to you. That kind of distraction can derail you."

She stood up, her hands on the splintered banister again. "That will be the biggest challenge." Then she smiled down at him. "But thanks for explaining things to me about why *you* came back. I don't think my reasons are nearly so clear-cut, but here I am."

"I didn't explain everything. There was a woman involved. She wanted more than I could give, so we parted ways. Took me a while to get my head straight. So just like you, here I am."

"Who would have thunk it, huh?"

He got up, shaking his head. "I guess we're the next generation."

"I guess so. Knotwood Mountain has lots of potential. I never planned to leave here. I was just kind of driven away. And I thought I'd never be able to come back. But this opportunity came along at the right time."

"And so now you're back and you seem to have a lot of potential yourself," he said before he could hold back. Then he turned to get back to work. Even a good distraction was still a distraction, after all. "I guess I'll see you out here a lot, considering how I deal with women every day in the store and I have one very temperamental mother. I know how many hissy fits a woman can throw."

"You got that right," she said. "I'm pretty sure this won't be my last one. I'm waiting to hear from the contractor then I'm going begging at the bank. If I can't get a loan for an overhaul, I guess I'll just fix up the downstairs and open for business. Start out small and work my way up, hopefully."

Rick took in that bit of information. He had connections down at the bank, but Cari would be insulted if he offered his help. Still, he wanted to help. "Good luck," he said, his mind spinning as he watched her head back inside.

Then his cell phone rang. "Hello?"

"Rick, how you doing?"

"Jolena, what's up?"

"I need to talk to you. About a mutual friend."

"Oh, yeah, and who's that?"

"Cari Duncan," Jolena replied. "I've got a plan but I need your help."

"Name it," Rick said, wondering what Jolena had up her sleeve. And wondering why her timing always seemed to be just right.

When he heard her idea, he had to smile. This just might work and if it did, Cari would have to go along with it. She'd be crazy not to.

Chapter Four

Cari sat down with the bank officer, her palms sweaty, her breath held. Feeling the cool bump of the old leather chair against her legs, she waited for her fate, a sensation of ultimate doom sifting in her stomach. "So, Mr. Phillips, what's the verdict?"

The older gray-haired man stared through his bifocals at her, his stern expression and apologetic discomfort shouting out the answer she already knew. Clearing his throat, he glanced down at the papers in front of him. "Well, young lady, you seem to have a long history here. Lots of credit problems." He put the papers down and leaned back in his squeaky chair, the tuffs of peppered hair on the top of his head looking like twisted fence wire.

"Carinna, I have to be honest with you. It doesn't look good. Especially in this economy. Any kind of business loan is risky these days, but this…well…the boutique idea is a good one and it worked for you in Atlanta, but while we always want to help new businesses here in Knotwood Mountain, financing a major renovation of that old house, well, that's just not something we're ready to do, I'm afraid."

"But you've seen my business plan," she said, ready to fight for herself. "It's solid, based on my success in Atlanta. I've paid off most of my credit card debt and I even have some start-up money saved. I know it's not much, but I'm willing to do a lot of the work myself to save money."

"What about your projections? We need to be sure you can make your monthly payments."

"My cash flow projections are low, but I did a conservative estimate on that. I fully expect business to pick up once I get some advertising out there. I'll find a way to pay back the loan." She hoped.

"All good points, but you don't have anything for collateral. Or anyone willing to cosign on this."

Cari didn't like his condescending tone or the implication that she didn't have another soul willing to take a risk on her. "I have the house sitting on a prime corner lot on First Street. That should be collateral enough."

"Not in this day and time," he replied, his ink pen thumping against his desk pad. "But you could probably sell it for a tidy sum and start over in some other location within the town. Your stepmother could help you there, I'm sure."

Cari sat still, refusing to have a meltdown in front of this grumpy old man. She'd done her homework, learned all about small business loans, talked to her financial advisor about the risks. She'd even joined the Small Business Association and found lots of online tips. And there was the slight possibility of getting grant money if she registered the house as a historical landmark.

All of that aside, it seemed this man was going to be her biggest obstacle, because he controlled the purse strings. But, she reminded herself, he was just doing his job. "I understand, Mr. Phillips. And I was shocked at the amount the contractor quoted me on the renovations, too. What if I did a little bit at a time? I don't have to do everything he's suggesting. I can just get the bottom floor updated and in working order so I can open my boutique. If I have it up and running before the Fourth, I know I'll clear enough to make the monthly loan payments as the year goes by. Christmas is always a good season here, too, with the winter tourists."

"You can't predict that," he replied, taking off his glasses. "Look, I knew your father. He was a solid businessman—knew a good piece of real estate when he saw it. Maybe he left you Duncan House so you could sell the whole thing and turn a nice profit. It's in an ideal location for a new business."

"Just not the new business I'm proposing," Cari replied, disappointment coloring her words.

"I'm afraid so. I can't lend you money on your name alone, although the bank did take that into consideration."

"But my good name just isn't enough, is it?" she asked, her finger hitting the report in front of him. "I got myself into a financial mess. But I worked hard over the last couple of years to straighten things out. My business plan worked in Atlanta. I just let my personal finances get out of control."

"It takes longer than a couple of years to

clear up bad credit and you know it," he retorted. "I do admire your fortitude, however."

Cari stood, her fingers grasping the strap of her bag. "And I admire your complete and unwavering honesty. But I'm not going to give up on this. I came to you first because this is where my father did his banking. I'll just try somewhere else."

"You'll have a tough row to hoe, Carinna. I wish you luck."

Cari turned to leave, dignity and the Duncan name making her spine straight. Too bad she hadn't considered coming to the bank *before* moving into the old house. But she wanted to live there, remodel or no remodel. She'd find a way to make this work, if she had to redo the house in square yard increments. And if she had to find a job somewhere else until she could get the boutique going.

She was on her way out the double doors when they swooshed open, the morning heat and sunshine warring with the sterile air-conditioning and doom and gloom of the annoying bank. Cari looked up and found herself blocked by Jolena and—

"Hi, Rick, what are you doing here?"

"He's with me," Jolena said, lifting a thumb toward Rick. "I mean, we're together—here to see you." She looked past Cari to Mr. Phillip's office. "Let's go back in and talk to the man, honey."

"What?" Cari tried to protest, but Rick's strong hand on her elbow stopped her. When he guided her back toward the big office, she asked, "What's going on?"

"We have a plan," Rick said, not bothering to slow down. "Just be quiet and listen."

Not sure she liked being ordered around, even if he did look yummy and forceful in his white shirt and crisp jeans, Cari glanced from Jolena to Rick. "Jo, what's about to happen?"

"You getting your loan approved," Jolena replied, her dark eyes wide with intrigue and triumph. "Let Rick do the talking, okay?"

Cari didn't have much choice. Rick was already shaking hands with Mr. Phillips. What were they going to do, hold a gun on the man and demand he give her some money? Not a half-bad idea, although that would look like bank robbery to all the other customers.

"This is…highly unusual," Mr. Phillips said, his expression bordering on perturbed. "Rick, care to explain this unexpected visit?"

Rick directed Cari to a chair and gently pushed her down. "Yes, sir. Mrs. Beasley and I are here as concerned citizens of Knotwood Mountain. Since we're both business owners on First Street and since Miss Duncan wants to renovate Duncan House and move her already successful business here, and since she is the daughter of one of the town's most prominent citizens—now deceased—we're here to make you an offer you can't refuse."

Both Cari and Mr. Phillips asked the same question. "Which is?"

Jolena grinned and nodded toward Rick. "Tell him, Rick. Go ahead."

Rick pressed his hands onto the big desk, his knuckles splayed across the unfortunate report regarding Cari's finances. "We want to cosign a loan for Cari Duncan."

"What?" Cari gasped, shaking her head.

"Impossible," Mr. Phillips retorted.

"Not so quick," Rick said, finally sitting down to talk business. "Think about this. Jolena and I both have a vested interest in the upkeep of First Street, and let's face it, Duncan House had been an eyesore for years now. While we appreciate that Cari's father was ill for many of those years and that his wife, Doreen, did her best to run his real estate company, we couldn't help but notice the second Mrs. Duncan tended to neglect Duncan House."

He gave Cari an encouraging look. "It's been vacant for over a year now and, well, it just doesn't sit well with us that the house has become so unappealing and run-down." He sat up, his tone going from conversational to serious. "It doesn't sit well with the chamber of commerce or the city council either. And I'm sure it doesn't impress the locals and the tourists, not at all. I get complaints on a daily basis."

Mr. Phillips lifted a hand. "But—"

Rick went right on talking. "I've thought of buying the place myself, but you know I have my hands full with the general store. And Jolena has a good thing going with the diner, but her customers have to stare at that boarded-up old house all the time. And that's a shame."

"A real crying shame," Jolena added, her chin bobbing.

"Why, just the other day, Mrs. Meadows asked me what we intended to do about that old house. And when I told her none other than little Cari Duncan herself, the daughter of James Duncan, was coming back to fix up the place, well, I can't tell you how excited

Mrs. Meadows was. She even said she'd get the Garden Club in on helping with the landscaping. Something about getting the place on the National Historic Registry, too. And you know she's one of those Daughters of the Revolution—those women can sure stir up a stink when they want something done. And Mrs. Meadows really wants something done about Duncan House. But only if she knows someone is willing to invest in the renovations. And do them up proper, of course."

"But—"

Rick went in for the kill. "No buts, just a good solid plan to keep First Street pristine and tourist-ready. That's why we're here, Mr. Phillips. To do our civic duty."

Cari tried to speak. "But—"

"No buts," Jolena said, elbowing her in the ribs. "Work with us here, suga'."

"I can't let y'all do this," Cari said, trying to stand. Two strong hands grabbed her and put her back in her place.

"Yes, you can," Rick replied. "Because we're not actually doing this for you— although we like you and we're glad you're back. It's for the overall good of this community." He winked at her then turned back to Mr. Phillips. "I'd hate to have to take this matter before the city council later this month. You know how revved up those good old boys can get when they think we're losing tourist dollars."

Mr. Phillips looked like a whipped puppy. "This is highly unusual and a bit unortho-dox."

Jolena let out a bubbling giggle. "It's all about a good cause, Mr. Phillips. Just think what a glowing report we could give for the bank, knowing that you took a risk on a hometown girl and her dreams? Her daddy would be so proud. And I'm sure it will make a favorable impression on others who might want to do business with you."

Rick nodded. "Cari gets the loan and we both cosign as collateral. If things don't work out and she can't pay, Jolena and I will take over the payments and co-own the property then we'll decide what to do with it. How's that for a solid plan?"

"I just don't know," Mr. Phillips said.

But Cari could see the wheels spinning in his head. The man knew he was sitting across from two prominent members of the commu-nity, two people with a lot of pull and power. Two people with determined looks and a lot of name-dropping to back those looks. As surprised and shocked as she was, Cari was glad to have them in her corner. Not sure if she should be thankful or full of denial and refusal, she had to speak up.

"I can't allow this," she said. "I just can't."

"You don't have any other choice," Mr. Phillips said. "If these two are willing to take the risk then I guess I'm willing to loan you the money. But not the whole amount, Cari. I'll give you fifty thousand to get you started—that's half, and that's generous for a small-business loan. If you fail, your friends here will be out twenty-five thousand each. Unless you can find a way to salvage this crazy plan."

Cari couldn't breathe. She'd just gone from being broke and with no hope to having money and a lot of new hope. But it would mean she owed Jolena a great deal. And Rick Adams, too.

Was she so pathetic that the best-looking man in town felt sorry for her? Sorry enough to float her a loan? That didn't make a bit of sense, but it was so sweet. Wasn't it?

"I don't know," she said, shaking her head. "I wanted to do this on my own."

"You will be doing it on your own, honey," Jolena said, her hand touching Cari's. "It's a loan from the bank—and that's what you needed. We're just the insurance policy. And we talked this over good and thorough and we both agree you won't let us down."

Before Cari could form another protest, the handshake agreement was in place and the paperwork was being drawn up.

"You can all meet back here in a few days to sign the papers," Mr. Phillips said, smiling at last. He reached out a hand to Rick. "Good doing business with you."

Rick pointed to Cari. "You're doing business with this woman, Mr. Phillips. She's the boss. Don't forget that."

Cari appreciated the way he'd shifted the power back to her. But she wanted to have a long talk with him when she could find her pulse again.

"Thank you, Mr. Phillips," she finally said. "I'll be in touch."

The old man nodded and gave her a grudging smile. "You must be a lot like your father, Cari. He always had champions, friends willing to vouch for him no matter what. That's how he formed such a solid business." He glanced down at his desk and mumbled, "Too bad his current wife can't be the same way." Looking embarrassed, he quickly amended that. "But it seems *you* have two very high-up champions of your own. Not a bad way to start out, let me tell you."

Jolena pointed a finger toward the ceiling. "She has one very, very high-up champion— the Lord wants Cari to grow and prosper. I think that's why He brought her home."

"I can't fight that kind of power," Mr. Phillips replied with a grin. "Now, if y'all don't mind, I do have some *scheduled* appointments today."

Cari waited until they walked out onto the sidewalk before she turned on them. "I can't believe you two. You steamrolled me into this. Now I not only owe the bank, but I owe both of you, too."

"A simple thank-you would be nice," Jolena said, giving her a stern look.

"Thank you," she said, letting out a long breath. "But honestly, I don't know how to thank you. I feel like a charity case."

"You are no such thing," Rick replied. "Jolena and I had a long talk and decided this would be a good business decision. Doreen purposely let that house go to ruin. This is our way of taking care of business. So don't go all noble and self-righteous on us. We intend to see a return on our investment, let me tell you."

Jolena chimed in. "Yeah. Our best hope is that we never have to take over that loan, honey. While we'd love to own rental property on First Street, we'd rather just sign off and be done with it when push comes to shove."

"No pressure there," Cari said, wondering how she'd managed to get herself in this fix. "But I am grateful. I can't begin to tell you what this means to me."

Jolena gave her a quick hug. "I've got work to do." Then she leaned close. "Your parents gave me a start twenty years ago. They sold me the diner at a rock-bottom price and even did owner financing for me. I owe them both, honey. This is my way of paying back a grateful debt."

A grateful debt. Cari liked that concept. And she was grateful. "I'll work hard to make sure I do the same, then."

She watched as Jolena pranced down the flower-lined street toward the diner. Then Cari turned to Rick. "Okay, I get why Jolena helped me. She's obligated since she's my godmother. But you, Rick? I don't understand that part. You barely know me. Care to explain why you just put your neck on the line for me?"

He started to speak, but she interrupted him. "And don't give me that good-business-good-neighbor-good-for-the-community speech, even though it's a very persuasive speech. Just tell me why you'd take a chance on me like this? I'm thankful and I'm humbled, and I'm going to work hard to show you how much I appreciate this. But I really need to know why you stood up for me in there. What's in it for you?"

Chapter Five

Rick couldn't believe what she'd just asked him. "What do you mean, what's in it for me? You make it sound as if I deliberately bullied you into getting your loan because I had a hidden agenda."

"Well, you sorta did, didn't you?"

Wondering if he had made a mistake—a big one—he couldn't decide if she was thrilled that she had a chance to fix up Duncan House or if she detested him for trying to help. "You don't trust me, do you?"

"It's not that. Okay, maybe I just don't trust your motives. We haven't seen each other since high school. And we weren't exactly chummy back then."

He hit his head with his hand then scrubbed

it down his face. "You can't be serious? You think I have ulterior motives?"

"Do you?"

Rick grunted, trying to think of a retort. "I called myself trying to help another human being. Who messed you up this much?"

She shifted, throwing that ridiculously large leather bag over her shoulder. "Okay, so I have trust issues. I trusted my father and look where that got me. I've had one bad relationship after another and I almost went to the poorhouse just trying to impress the last man I dated. You'd think I'd run screaming from any man who offers me help. And yet, here I stand, taking handouts on the street." She shrugged then let out a long breath. "I came back here to learn to stand on my own two feet. And already, I've been rescued. Do you know how that makes me feel?"

So that was it. She was shielding herself by second-guessing him and accusing him. Maybe because he'd embarrassed her by springing this on her? "Hey, this is *not* a handout and I didn't do this to rescue you. You've had some tough breaks so Jolena and I wanted to give you a fair start by backing you on this one thing. But if you feel that way just march right back over to the bank and tell old man Phillips you don't want his money. It'll sure be a big worry off my mind."

She stared up at him with those iridescent eyes, her humility clear on her tightly drawn face. Rick watched as she frowned then looked down at her gladiator sandals, her freckled skin blushing a becoming red. "I'm so stupid," she finally mumbled. "Look, Rick, I don't mean to sound horrible and unappreciative. What you just did in there for me is so incredible, but it's hard to believe."

He shouldn't have fussed at her, but at least she was calming down a little bit. "Is it so hard to believe that people around here are willing to help other people?"

"Yes," she said, nodding her head. "Yes, it is. I left here broken and afraid—an outcast—and I missed my father so much. I couldn't come back though. I just couldn't. I guess I built this protective shell around myself. And I forgot what real kindness is all about. I'm sorry. So sorry."

Rick wished he hadn't been so impulsive and harsh with her. "Look, it's okay. Maybe we should have discussed the plan with you before ambushing you at the bank. You think it's charity but it's not. It's just a cosign on a loan. A business decision. You don't owe me anything and I don't expect you to grovel every time you see me."

She actually grinned at that, her features relaxing. "I never planned on groveling. Maybe baking you a pie or something—even if I can't cook very well."

"You could just buy me a pie from Jolena. I love her strawberry icebox pies."

"That I can do, whenever my loan comes through that is."

He reached out to shake her hand. "Then we're square, you and me?"

"I guess so. It's just so odd, knowing you helped me like this."

"Oh, I cosign loans with a lot of the women I meet. It's just my way of doing things. And it's a great way to break the ice."

She slapped at his arm, her smile genuine. "You make me laugh. How is that possible?"

"Because I'm a clown? Maybe a clown with little forethought on some things?"

"No, because you're a good, sweet man. An old acquaintance, but new friend. And it's been a long time since I've had a friend I could really trust."

He had to laugh at that quick turnaround. "Oh, so you trust me now?"

"Yes, I do. I don't know why, but I do." She

moved away. "Do you trust me—to make good on that loan?"

"I'm going to try. It'll be mighty hard explaining to my mom and brother if you don't. I don't know how they'd go for being co-owners of Duncan House."

Her eyes widened. "You didn't discuss this with them?"

Rick grimaced. He hadn't meant to let that slip. "We didn't have time, and besides, I don't discuss a lot of what I do with them. They both tend to lean on me for the big decisions. And with this, it was today or never at the bank. Jolena and I had to move fast, especially when we saw you coming out of the bank, looking disappointed."

Because she looked so worried now, he said, "Hey, I have a hefty sum of money at that bank. Mr. Phillips knows that. It's okay. I sold a lot of my stock and set up some certificates of deposit when I moved back here. All of my investments flow through the bank, so they owe me one."

"You never cease to amaze me," she replied. "You are a smart businessman. I can learn from that."

"I can't complain," he said. "But if I don't get back to the store, my mom's gonna send out the stock boy to find me. Even smart businessmen still have to answer to their mothers sometimes."

She hesitated then smiled at him. "Thanks again. I mean it. I won't forget what you did." Slanting her head to one side, she said, "I guess this makes us partners in a way, right?"

Rick hadn't considered that angle. "I guess it does at that. But I'm more of a silent partner. Now, Jolena, that's a whole 'nother thing."

She smiled again. "I can handle Jolena. And I owe you both a big debt of gratitude."

When she reached out her hand, he took it, shaking it with businesslike precision. And with an acute awareness of how tiny and dainty her fingers felt against his.

She must have felt the same strong current. Her eyes lifted to meet his, surprise pooling inside their depths.

Rick let go then started walking backward toward the store. "Maybe, just maybe, you can reward me for my good deed one day."

"Oh, yeah. How's that?"

"By wearing those red shoes. I'm going to save them just for you—size seven. Sort of like a housewarming gift."

"Hey, how do you know my size?"

"I have my sources," he said, grinning at the pretty glow in her eyes. "See you later, Princess."

Her laughter echoed after him, making him glad he'd stepped up to help her. Cari was a nice woman. Maybe she just needed someone to show her that same nice so she'd recognize it in herself.

A few days later, Cari was busy unpacking the rest of the stuff she'd brought from Atlanta. She'd sold off most of her furniture and a lot of her clothes. She'd kept only what she could put in her midsize economy sedan and a small rental trailer hitched to her car. Since she couldn't do much upstairs right now besides sleep, she put her old leather love seat in what used to be the dining room, across from the big parlor that would serve as the main space for her shop.

The big bay window had a window box, so she cleaned and scrubbed that inside out to make sure no cobwebs or other critters were inside. She stored some clothes and books there for now. A couple of chintzy chairs she'd salvaged from a garage sale and re-covered finished the make-do room. Thankfully the windows had drapery—old and ugly—but the bright blue heavy curtains did allow her some privacy at night and they picked up the blue flowers in the chairs.

After she'd tidied up her temporary sleeping quarters upstairs by placing a favorite quilt over the air mattress and setting out an old fern stand for a nightstand, she tackled the small downstairs bath again, hoping to add some flowers and a couple of botanical prints to make the room brighter. It had been installed long after the original house was built in what must have been a storage closet in a long hallway, but the plumbing worked fairly well if she remembered to jiggle the handles on everything. She'd just finished scrubbing it down for the third time and putting out some toiletries when she heard footsteps hitting the porch.

Peeking up the hallway, Cari saw a teenage boy peering inside the beveled glass on the old front door.

She hurried up the hallway then cracked open the door. "Can I help you?"

"Cari?"

It took her a minute. A familiar sensation swept over her as she stared at the young man. His blond hair was long and shaggy and his blue eyes wide with a hopefulness that tugged at her heart. "Brady?"

He grinned. "Yeah. Can I come in?"

"Of course." She opened the door and instantly hugged him close, tears forming in her eyes. "You've gotten so big."

He stood back, obviously uncomfortable with the hugging situation. "I was only eight when you left. I'm sixteen now. I just got my driver's license."

"You're driving. Oh, wow."

Her stepbrother had grown up. She called him her stepbrother even though she'd only lived in her father's house for a couple of years after he'd married Doreen. But she'd been the built-in babysitter during that time and while Brady's sister Bridget had been a brat at fourteen, Brady had been a confused little boy who needed some attention.

"Mom doesn't know I'm here," he said, looking down at his big feet. "I just wanted to say hi."

"I'm glad you came by. Want a soda?"

He nodded then glanced around. "I can't believe you're gonna live in this old place. You know Mom hates this house."

"Yeah, I kind of gathered that," Cari replied, careful not to say anything derogatory about Doreen to her son. "I've always loved it, I guess because I grew up here. I felt like a princess living in a big castle." But she'd learned that fairy tales were just that—tales that never had a happy ending in reality.

Brady slung his shaggy hair off his face. "Bridget thinks it's lame, you living here. She listens to whatever Mom says. And Mom isn't happy about it. She wanted to keep this property and sell it for a profit or something like that."

Cari let that slide as she reached into her ice chest and took out a drink. "How's Bridget? Is she off to college yet?"

He popped the top and took a swig of his soda. "She was in school but she flunked out, only Mom doesn't want anybody to know that. She's home for the summer. I don't see her much so I don't know if she's going back to school. She likes to hang with her friends and party a lot." He rolled his eyes. "And she has like this major crush on your neighbor next door."

Cari furrowed her brow. "Who's that?"

"Rick Adams," he said. "Have you met him? That older dude who runs the general store? Mr. Goody Two-shoes—always doing something to 'help give back' as he calls it. Bridget thinks he's so all that. She's always going in there to buy stuff so she can flirt with him. Mom tells her he's a *fine catch,* whatever that means."

Cari's heart did a strange flip. Trying to wrap her mind around Bridget and Rick as a couple, she decided she'd have to withhold judgment until she actually saw Bridget. "A bit young for him, don't you think?"

"She likes older men. Especially men who can buy her things."

"Oh, I see."

She did see. Bridget had always been self-centered and shallow and it sounded as if that hadn't changed. The younger girl had taken Cari's place in James Duncan's affection. Cari had witnessed that right from the start. Remembering her pretty blue sandals, she wondered how many pairs of shoes Bridget had now. It didn't really matter, except for the principle of the thing. It wasn't fair but then, she'd learned that a lot of things in life were not fair. Besides, what Rick did with his spare time was his business.

Did he return Bridget's affections?

Putting that burning question out of her mind, she focused on Brady. "Hey, I was about to get a bite to eat over at Jolena's. Want to come?"

Brady looked hesitant at first then finally

bobbed his head. "I could go for a burger, yeah."

"Okay then. Let me shut things down here and we'll walk over."

He waited for her to grab her purse and cell phone. "So you're gonna open a shop here? Mom said it sounded like junk to her."

Cari gritted her teeth at that remark. "Not junk." She wasn't in the mood to keep explaining. "I design things—and redesign other things. Plus, I go to market and find clothes and accessories that I know women will love. It's fun and I did pretty good back in Atlanta."

Until the rent went up in the quaint little shop where she'd been for three years and her ex-boyfriend drained most of her bank account because he'd lost his own job. But Brady wouldn't be interested in all that. No one was interested in hearing a hard-luck story from this particular princess.

"I have to come up with a name for my shop. Got any ideas?"

Brady shrugged and flipped his hair. "No. I guess it won't matter what you call the place. The chicks will love it."

"Chicks?" She pushed at his shoulder. "So are you into chicks?"

"Maybe." He grinned but didn't say anything else.

Cari glanced around at the tourists mingling here and there along the street. She needed to get in on some of this foot traffic. The village was gearing up for the summer festival, which would end with a big Fourth of July celebration in the town square. The crape myrtle lining the long street was blooming in dark pinks and vivid purples. The ancient magnolia trees were bursting with lemon-and-vanilla-scented white blossoms and the hydrangeas lining the park and square were fat with brilliant blue flowers that looked like pudgy sponges. All the merchants on the street had colorful potted plants by their doors and American flags flying in a symmetrical, solid row, giving a rainbow effect as the flags flapped in the breeze and the sun rays shimmered off the asphalt.

"It's good to be home," she said, glancing over at Brady. "A lot has changed since I left."

"Yeah, I'm glad you're back."

Smiling, she thought you couldn't get more Middle America than Knotwood Mountain. She'd always enjoyed the town festivals as a child. It would be so different, being involved as an adult and an actual local merchant. If only she could make this work. First, she'd plant her own container gardens with the cuttings Jolena had given her to root.

Finding roots. That's what she wanted and needed. Her father wasn't here anymore, but his shadow hung over everything she did. And she wanted him to know, to see, that she was trying so hard. She wanted that shadow to become a shield.

Please, Lord, I need Your help. I need guidance and self-control and a lot of patience. A whole lot of patience.

That last plea would certainly come in handy, she thought a few minutes later. After Cari and Brady found a booth by the big window of the diner, a bright white sports car zoomed up to the curb in front of the general store and skidded to a stop.

And out stepped Bridget Stillman, wearing a tight, short floral dress and high-heeled white sandals. Her long blond hair fell in delicate waves down her back as she exited the tiny car, a designer bag strapped around her wrist.

Brady glanced over at Cari then back out the window. "Right on time. She does that just about every afternoon. She's angling for a date with him."

Cari waited a beat then asked, "And does he ever take her up on that?"

Brady shrugged. "I've seen them walk over here together sometimes and a couple of times they've driven off in her car. Not my problem." He eyed the menu then grinned over at her. "I'm ready for that burger."

Cari nodded, focusing on the special of the day to keep from straining her gaze toward the general store. She'd buy Brady a burger, but her own appetite had disappeared in a puff of white car and shiny chrome, long blond hair and even longer shapely legs. It shouldn't bother her that Bridget was young, gorgeous and apparently living off the fruits of James Duncan's labor. Really it shouldn't bother her at all.

But it did. Which made her even more determined to become a success in the face of Doreen's obvious doubt and scorn. She'd have to work twice as hard to achieve about half as much success. She couldn't let Rick and Jolena down and she refused to let herself down. This would be hard, but it would be worth it. So worth it.

Maybe living well could be her best

revenge. And maybe forgetting about how Rick Adams made her smile could be her challenge for the day, or maybe for the rest of her life.

Chapter Six

Jolena ambled over to Cari's booth. "Well, look what we have here. It's been many a year since I've seen you two in here together." She glanced across the street at the sports car then rolled her eyes. "Everything okay?"

"Yes," Cari said, shooting Jolena a warning look. "Brady inhaled his burger."

"And what about you?" Jolena asked, eyeing Cari's half-eaten club sandwich. "Not hungry today?"

"I had one of your cinnamon rolls for breakfast," Cari said by way of explanation. "Still full."

"It's nearly dinnertime," Jolena shot back. "You can take the rest of this home for later."

Cari nodded and pushed her plate toward

Jolena. "I can't keep taking food from you, Jolena. I have to be a paying customer."

"Are you gonna get on that charity kick again?" Jolena asked, her tone low. "I'll keep a tab for you the way I do with Rick."

Cari looked over at Brady. The boy was absorbed in the last of his French fries. "I appreciate that and I will pay up. We had this conversation on the phone, remember? Right after you swooped in and saved my bacon at the bank the other day. I'd say that's enough, tab or no tab."

Jolena chuckled. "I get it, honey. But I don't mind feeding you either. You're family. It's that simple."

Cari was touched by Jolena's declaration. "Thanks."

After Jolena winked at her then walked away with the remains of her meal, she watched Brady finish his fries. Did she have any family left? Her grandparents were all dead and her father and mother had both been only children. No aunts, uncles or even cousins that she knew of. Maybe Jolena was right. Maybe Cari had to create her own family now that she was alone.

Staring over at Brady, she decided at least she could keep close to him. He didn't seem to mind that she wasn't on his mother's Christ-mas-card list. Maybe, just like her, he needed a friend, someone to talk to now and then.

"Brady, do you and your sister go to church?" she asked, thinking she needed to do that very thing herself. Her mother had always told her that the church was where you found the community.

He shrugged. "I do sometimes when something cool's going on in Youth. Bridget never goes. She sleeps too late every Sunday."

"And your mom?"

"Oh, she goes. But only to look for clients and to 'network' as she calls it. She sits right up there at the front."

"Of course," Cari replied, hoping the acid in her tone didn't sound too sizzling.

"Do you go?"

"I haven't since I got here last week. Maybe I'll see you there this coming Sunday."

He frowned. "Yeah, whatever."

That attitude didn't bode well, Cari thought. But since she'd had the same attitude for years now, maybe she should sit up and take notice herself. "Well, I enjoyed having this late lunch with you. I hope you'll come by and see me again."

He looked out the window. "I will. I like having stuff to do. I try to stay out of Mom's hair."

"I could use some help fixing up the house," she said. "You saw how big those high-ceilinged rooms are. It's gonna take me at least a week of steady work to get the rooms I want to use for the boutique painted and decorated. But I want to do some of it myself to save money."

"I haven't done much painting but I'm willing to try," he said. "I have some buddies who might want to help out, if that's okay."

"Sure. The more the merrier. Do you have a girlfriend?"

He looked sheepish. "Kinda. Just a good friend."

"That works," she replied, her attention wandering across the street. "Friendship has merit."

And that's when she saw them—Rick and Bridget—emerging from the general store, laughing and talking.

And they were headed right for the diner.

"Oh, it's getting late," she said to Brady. "I guess I'd better get back over to the house."

"Oh, okay." He drained his soda then hopped up. "Thanks for the food."

"Sure. Come by next week and we'll see about training you to paint."

He nodded then turned toward the door, but he took off in the opposite direction of his sister and Rick—not that they even bothered looking up. In fact, a moving truck could have easily come barreling up the street toward them and they wouldn't have noticed.

Cari thought about ducking out the back, but Jolena blocked her where she stood. "Don't go running now. What did your mama teach you about being a lady?"

Cari made a face. "Not to trip up pretty girls in short dresses who've taken advantage of my deceased father's good graces?" Glaring out the window, she eyed Bridget. "Bless her little heart."

"That would be one part of the lesson."

"Oh, all right. I have to face obstacles with my head held high and a sweet smile plastered on my face." She smiled, big and bright. "How's this?"

"As fake as plastic petunias but it's a start." Jolena nodded toward the door. "That girl ain't got nothing on you, baby. You're a Duncan, remember?"

"Yes, ma'am." Cari fluffed her hair and stood firm, her shoulders back. "Bring it on, Blondie."

Jolena let out another chuckle as the bells on the door chimed when it swooshed open. "Rick Adams, did you come back for more of my strawberry pie?"

Rick tore his gaze away from Bridget then glanced at Cari in surprise. "Hello, ladies. Bridget wanted some lemonade."

"So Rick was sweet enough to keep me company," she said, her sights trained on Cari. Giving Cari a dismissive once-over, she said, "I heard you were back."

Cari waited then realized that was all she was going to get. "Yes, I am. And I'm very busy. Just came over for a bite to eat. I saw Brady. He sure has grown."

Bridget twirled her hair and lifted one elegant eyebrow. "That brat. He's whining for a new car, but Mom says he has to wait until he has his for-real driver's license." Then she lifted the other brow. "What was he doing hanging around with you?"

Cari glanced at Rick to see if the same distaste Bridget so obviously had for her had rubbed off on him. He looked embarrassed but his expression went into panic mode, followed by what looked like an I-can-explain mode.

Hoping to protect Brady, she said, "We just ran into each other. No harm done. It was good to see him. And you, too." She moved to leave, hoping she didn't choke on that little fib, but Bridget just stood there, blocking her way. Giving Rick a quick glance, Cari said, "Excuse me."

Rick pulled Bridget out of the way. "See you later, Cari."

Cari didn't answer. Her skin burned with the heat of humiliation as she hurried across the street. She didn't dare look back or hope that Rick would come after her. Why should he? They were just friends, plain and simple if she didn't count the fact that he'd agreed to cosign a loan with her.

While he carried on with her stepsister right in front of her eyes.

What did she expect?

Once she was inside her house, she threw her bag on a nearby chair and walked straight through to the back of the house. She needed privacy and air. And today, she needed to escape, but Rick might find her on the porch. So she headed upstairs, careful to make her way to the turret room. Watching where she stepped, she managed to find a clean spot on the old octagon window seat. And she sat there, looking out through one of the broken windowpanes, wondering why what used to be her sanctuary now felt like her prison. She didn't need to count on anyone for anything, really. She couldn't.

She needed to remember that Rick Adams owed her nothing. Nothing at all. He still was and would always be the blond-haired-long-legged-cheerleader type. Not her type, not even on the radar. Except to hand out favors and make her laugh.

She'd have to accept that Rick was a business acquaintance and a silent partner in a unique business deal. She'd just have to settle for that.

But that would be the only thing she'd settle for.

Rick gave Jolena a pleading look then glanced out the door, watching Cari's retreating figure as she practically ran across the street. Jolena shot him a penetrating, not-so-pleased look but kept her cool. Torn between going after Cari or just minding his own business, he was a man trapped.

And being a typical man, he did nothing

to lessen that situation. For now. He'd talk to Cari later. After he managed to get away from Bridget.

"I'll get someone to bring your lemonades," Jolena said, turning so fast her braided hair did a dance around her shoulders.

Bridget seemed oblivious to the undercurrents, Rick noted. But then, Bridget was pretty much oblivious to everyone and everything around her. Shrugging, she giggled. "Cari sure left in a hurry. I think if you'd said 'Boo' she would have fainted. She always was a little skittish around men." Her smile indicated that she, on the other hand, did not have a problem with men.

And why had he let her drag him over here when he had so much to do before closing time in less than an hour?

"Cut her some slack," he said after they'd settled onto bar stools at the counter. Glad there weren't many customers in the diner this time of day, he willed the waitress to hurry with the lemonade. Thankfully, the young girl came right up with two tall plastic cups brimming with sliced lemons and crushed ice. "Cari's had it rough lately."

"So I hear," Bridget said before she slurped

her drink. "But, you know, she brought it all on herself. I mean, she always, always caused trouble with her daddy, and he was such a sweet old man—most of the time. Then she went off and got herself all in a mess, money wise. Mama says Cari couldn't manage her money if Ben Franklin himself was sitting right beside her."

Rick watched as Jolena marched toward them, her eyes burning with all the signs to do feminine battle. "I have to get back to work, Bridget. Walk with me."

He grabbed his drink with one hand and her skinny arm with the other. "Thanks, Jolena. Put it on my tab."

"Uh-huh," Jolena said with a grunt. "You'd better pay up on that tab real soon."

Rick knew a threat when he heard one. He was so in hot water. And honestly, he wasn't sure what he'd done to bring this on. Except walk across the street with Bridget, of course. He should have remembered how territorial women could be. And that they never ever let go of a grudge.

Bridget pulled away from him when they were outside. "Hey, I thought we were going to have a nice, quiet talk before you took me out to dinner."

Rick silently counted to ten then prayed for patience. "And I thought we were just getting a quick drink before I got back to work."

She actually stomped her foot. "But dinner, remember? You keep promising and then you always cancel out at the last minute."

How to make her understand? "Bridget, I've never promised you dinner." In fact, he'd never once asked her out to dinner, for that matter. She did the asking and the finagling and tried her level best to manipulate him into a meal. Which he always managed to graciously refuse. Or so he thought. Maybe he was just too nice for his own good. His mother always told him he had a hard time turning away from a pretty, pouting face. And he had the battle scars to prove it, didn't he?

But back to pretty, pouting faces. Bridget had cornered the market on that particular tactic. "Look, I can't go to dinner with you. I have to go out to my ranch and check on the livestock." And find a few quiet hours for himself. No wonder his brother was so reclusive.

Her eyes sparkled with a new plan. "I could go with you. I've never even seen your dusty old ranch. We could go horseback riding then build a campfire."

Rick saw the romantic hope in her baby blues. Trying hard to think of a kind way to extract himself, he said, "My mom's coming with me to visit my brother. And you know Simon doesn't like to be disturbed."

She leaned close, her heavy floral perfume making his nose twitch. "I wouldn't bother your big brother, I promise. I'd focus all of my attention on you."

Once not so long ago, Rick would have been tempted by that flirtatious offer. Once. But he'd changed since then, learned a few things about the female mind-set. And he'd been burned so badly, he was still gun-shy. So why had he allowed Bridget to keep flirting with him and why had he decided getting a cold lemonade with the woman was a good idea, especially when he'd ran smack into Cari and her obvious disapproval in the process?

Because sometimes, in spite of his best intentions, he fell back into the old habits.

Calling out in a silent plea to Heaven, he waited for a few minutes then regained his composure. "Bridget, I can't. I just can't, okay?"

Her sweetness and light turned to anger and darkness in a flutter of overly made-up eyelashes and a twist of tightly held pink lips. "Oh, all right then. Forget it. I've got other plans anyway." And with that, she tossed her still-full lemonade into the nearest trash can and pranced to her convertible. Before Rick could turn around, she was peeling out onto the street in a blur of shining white that caused the crape myrtle to bend in the wind.

That was unpleasant, he thought. He looked around, hoping no one had witnessed that little scene.

And saw a face staring down at him from the turret room of Duncan House. A face full of regret and disapproval. Cari's pretty, perturbed face.

Rick watched as she quickly disappeared from the old, broken window, thinking she really did look a lot like a princess trapped in a castle.

His throat dry, he finished off his lemonade and went back inside to his work, wishing he could figure out women.

And wishing he could explain to one woman in particular that he wasn't as shallow and despicable as she seemed to think he was, in spite of his actions to the contrary.

Chapter Seven

A few days later, Cari had just settled down to get some serious paperwork out of the way when a loud knock came at the door. For a small town, this place sure had a lot of foot traffic. That would certainly come in handy when she was open for business. When she opened the door, a petite young woman stood there holding a large crystal vase full of lilies, orchids and tulips.

"Hi, I'm Christie, from Knotwood Florist around the corner. Delivery for Cari Duncan."

"That's me," Cari said, her hands going to her mouth. "What beautiful flowers. Are you sure you got the right address?"

"They're for *you*—Cari Duncan," the girl said, clearly excited. "Look at the colors—

I've never seen so many shades of red and pink. And the white lilies—perfect. We rarely get such a big, specific order."

That word *perfect* stuck inside Cari's throbbing head. She stared at the flowers Christie held with such pride. "Is there a card?"

"Oh, yes," Christie said, clapping her hands. "There. Read it out loud." The girl sure had a lot of enthusiasm for her job.

Cari couldn't help but smile at Christie's glee, but she couldn't share her joy. Instead, a deep shuddering dread centered itself inside her heart as she pulled the tiny card out of the envelope. She should be thrilled about receiving such pretty flowers, but her heart wasn't in it this morning. She'd been too busy trying to salvage her leftover bills. And she had a feeling these were "apologetic" flowers from a man she barely knew. A man she shouldn't be so mad at right now since it really wasn't her business who he shared lemonade with. And yet, her disappointment seemed to be coloring her every mood this morning.

"Read the card," Christie urged, her vested interest in this delivery cute if a bit annoying.

Cari set the flowers down on the window

box then opened the card. "'These reminded me of you,'" she read out loud, her hand going to her throat. "'All vibrant and brilliant—and very determined. Welcome home, Cari.'"

The message was signed "Rick."

"Rick Adams," Christie said with a dreamy expression glazing over her eyes. "He came in himself and picked them out. Wow, oh, wow. I wish he'd send me flowers."

"You're too young to wish such things," Cari retorted, then instantly regretted her words. But honestly, was every female in this town in love with the man? "I mean, one day you'll get flowers from a nice man, I'm sure."

Christie looked downright crestfallen. "Yes, a girl can dream, can't she?"

Cari wanted to tell her, no, a girl shouldn't dream. A girl should have a solid, realistic mind-set in both love and business. A girl shouldn't sit around waiting for some prince to come riding up the hill to rescue her. Cari should know since she'd kissed a few frogs. But she didn't have the heart to burst that very big bubble of sheer joy Christie seemed to be floating around in. "Yes, a girl can dream. And the flowers are beautiful."

Christie bobbed her head. "They are."

Then she frowned. "I know he's dreamy and all that, but I've never heard of *determined* flowers. What kind of man sends a message like that?"

Grabbing her wallet, Cari handed Christie a tip and gave her a verbal explanation, thinking this question-asking delivery girl wouldn't make it in the aloof, urban big city. "One who's even more determined than these flowers," she replied. "He thinks I'm going to fall for the tried-and-true method, apparently. Thanks for bringing them over."

"No problem," Christie said. Then she pointed a finger toward Cari. "I'll be watching you two."

Cari smiled and waved the girl down the steps then shut the door. "You and about half the town."

After Christie left, Cari let her fingers trail over the fat white lily blossoms. These flowers were a bright spot on a warm summer day. Just what she'd needed after coming face-to-face with both of her stepsiblings the other day. For some reason, she couldn't get seeing Rick with Bridget out of her mind though.

And she knew exactly what Rick's message meant. Tulips and lilies and orchids were no shrinking violets. They forced themselves from the ground into blossoming flowers. Hadn't she done pretty much the same thing when she'd finally found her footing and changed her life? Hadn't she come back home to stand firm against her stepmother? Was she truly blossoming here, or would she wilt back into that passive violet she'd once been?

Maybe Rick was trying to tell her something by giving her a subtle compliment. Or maybe he was just feeling guilty that he'd avoided her over the past couple of days, after he'd been seen hanging out with the enemy.

The enemy? Was that how she saw Doreen and her children? Or was this enemy of her own making? Hadn't she come here seeking revenge? Or would she wind up being miserable herself? How could she be happy if she had to constantly worry about this other family who'd swooped in and messed up her life?

Cari was so confused she couldn't be sure what her own motives were, or what Rick's motives were either, but for some strange reason this mix of flowers did make her smile in spite of her doubts and disappointments.

And that was very unsettling.

Even more unsettling, three hours later he called and left a message on her cell phone, asking her out to dinner that night. She had to wonder how he'd gotten her number, but then the man always managed to do things that surprised her.

Still, she wasn't going out to dinner with him, no matter how surprising he was.

"I'm not going, of course," Cari told Jolena as they tested paint samples later that day. Holding up a soft green sample card, she said, "I like this one for down here. I want to keep the color authentic to the Victorian era. What do you think?"

"I think you should go," Jolena replied as she squinted at the sample card.

"I was talking about the paint."

"I like the paint. But I love these pretty flowers. I think Rick has a thing for you, suga'."

"No, he has a thing for Bridget. He's just friends with me, and in typical male fashion, he's probably playing both of us."

Jolena tossed down the samples she'd been holding. "Rick is not that kind of man. Bridget throws herself at him and he's just too nice to tell her to back off."

"Too nice? Or too caught up?"

"He might be caught—in a trap. But Rick's too smart to fall for Bridget Duncan, let me tell you. He indulges her because he wants to witness to her. Of course, that girl ain't seen the doors of a church since she was in vacation Bible school as a kid. Rick knows that and he worries about her. That's all."

Cari wasn't convinced. "Are you sure? I mean, he left Atlanta for a reason. And you said it had to do with a woman. Maybe Bridget reminds him of that woman. She fits the bill. And he didn't seem to be witnessing anything remotely close to a come-to-Jesus talk the other day."

"He's subtle in his witness and ministry. And how do you know the bill?" Jolena countered, shaking her head.

"How do I know?" Cari's chuckle echoed throughout the house. "I remember from high school, for one thing. It just stands to reason that he'd still go after the same type. Bridget is gorgeous. Even I can see that. What chance do I have against that and the fact that she always managed to get the attention of every boy around her, especially the ones I liked. She was too young to notice Rick in high school but she's obviously making up for that now."

Jolena huffed a derisive breath. "She can prance around all she likes. I don't think Rick's gonna fall for that. And you—well, you need to lighten up and just go with things, honey. See what happens."

"I can't go with this, Jolena. I just got back to town and my first week has been full of enough surprises and pitfalls already. I have to be very careful."

Jolena pursed her lips then glanced around. "I've been giving this whole thing some thought and I think it might be a good idea—you and Rick."

Cari's heart did a funny flip. "And why would you think that? Other than you are so obviously trying to fix me up with the man?"

Jolena tapped her leather Mary Jane flats against the wooden floor. "Well, think about it. According to you, Rick has a certain type of woman he likes. But that type hasn't worked out so great for him. So maybe he needs to try a new type. Such as you. And maybe, just maybe, you need to let go of some of those preconceived notions about the man and try to make nice." She pointed to the flowers centered in the middle of the kitchen table. "The man sent you flowers, Cari. I'd say that's a very good sign."

Cari flipped through the paint samples. "I have to admit, the flowers got to me. They smell so good and they brighten up this old place. It's been a long time since anyone sent me flowers. But I think he sent them out of guilt, not anything anywhere near romantic."

"Then why did he call and ask you to dinner tonight?"

"Maybe because a certain someone gave him my phone number. And you probably demanded he take me to dinner, too. I must be the latest charity case around here."

Jolena put a hand on her hip. "Honey, I'm good but I'm not that good. Rick asked for your number but he called you on his own. I can't tell the man what to do. I can only guide you two toward each other."

"Oh, okay, so he called on his own. And left a message. Why didn't he just walk over here?"

"Maybe because he was afraid you wouldn't open the door?"

"I wouldn't have," she said. "I have things to do tonight." She thought really hard and realized she didn't have much to do except maybe read a book or watch a movie on the tiny television she'd brought with her. Or maybe unpack, clean the whole house for the tenth time and worry about how she was going to make all of this work. In a word, she had nothing going on tonight that couldn't wait.

Jolena figured that out, too. "Yes, like look at sample cards for paint. That's a real fun Friday night. You and Rick should go out and celebrate securing that loan. We did sign the papers this morning."

"Yes, you and I did. But Rick couldn't meet us at the bank. He had to come in later. Or so he said, according to Mr. Phillips. Typical male avoidance tactic."

"He got busy with a shipment and he had several demanding customers wanting to rent rafts and tubes. Not to mention those kayakers—they sure love riding the river." Jolena waved her hands in the air. "The man works day and night in that big old store. He could use a break."

"Or he's too chicken to face me after listening to Bridget trying to knock me down a peg or two."

Jolena nodded on that. "I did give him a little talk about that. Trust me, the man won't ever bring her in for lemonade again when you're on the premises of my diner." Then she continued on, "But if he's chicken, why would he send you flowers and ask you out to dinner?"

"Oh, I don't know," Cari said with a groan. "Maybe to soften me up so he'd have the courage to face me again, or maybe because he just feels sorry for poor little Cari. I don't know and I don't care. I can't do this, Jolena. I just can't."

"You mean you won't do it," Jolena retorted. "You are one stubborn woman. You know something? The only one feeling sorry for Cari around here is Cari."

Cari shook her head, shocked at that suggestion even if it did ring true. "No, like Rick's card said, I'm determined. I have one thing on my mind and that's getting Duncan House back in shape and making a go of my business."

"That's two things," Jolena pointed out.

"You know what I mean."

"Yes, I do," Jolena said, retreating for now. "But I want you to be happy. You could just try with Rick. Just get to know the man. Give him a chance, Cari. You've both been through a lot—bad relationships, the death of loved ones and trying to start over again. You two have so much in common, but you're both tip-toeing around things 'cause y'all think you'll get hurt all over again."

"All in due time," Cari said. "You have a valid case for *friendship*. But I can't go for anything else right now. I won't be ugly to him, but you're right. I don't want to get hurt again. Ever."

Jolena let out a breath. "Okay, then. I gotta go pick up the girls from dance class. You gonna be in church Sunday?"

"I hope to be," Cari replied. "I need to be."

"I hear that," Jolena retorted with a big grin. Then she winked at Cari. "Rick comes every Sunday."

"Of course he does. The man must be a saint."

"Far from it," Jolena said, moving toward the door. "He's just a good man waiting for a good woman."

Cari waved bye, then locked the door behind Jolena, thinking she couldn't be that woman. She was no saint herself and maybe that was the problem.

Maybe she'd never see herself as being good enough for any man. Especially one like Rick who attracted women the way honey attracted bees.

Too much time and energy, that's what he'd require.

And Cari didn't have much of either right now.

"Yes, definitely the pale green," she said, concentrating on her paint samples. The color was good for this big open room and the brand was affordable now that she had a line of credit at the bank.

A line of credit Rick had helped her obtain, she reminded herself. Was she being too hard on him? After all, she could tell from seeing Bridget that the girl knew how to operate around the opposite sex. How could she blame Rick for that?

Cari glanced out the window, watching the sun setting over the tip of the mountains peeking behind the buildings. The plump white blossoms of the mountain rhododendrons shimmered like fluffy cotton balls against the breeze. "Lord, am I wrong to judge him when I don't even know him—the real him—and after he's been so kind to me?"

Of course she was wrong. But she couldn't bring herself to call him and tell him that. She just needed some time to think and to sort this out. Deciding if she hurried she could make it to the paint store before it closed, she grabbed her stuff and headed out the door.

She'd start painting tonight. Just some scraping and testing, maybe put a primer on and then try the new color. Her contractor could work around that. Getting a head start would help her to think and it would also make her tired enough to sleep, she hoped. And since she'd set up her small television down here and the cable man had come by earlier to hook up reception, she might find an old movie to watch later. A good solid plan. A lonely, solitary plan, but a good one.

As she hurried out the front door, the scent of lilies drifted through the air, reminding her that she could have had a date tonight. A real date with a real man.

Cari shut the door and got in her car before she had time to change her mind and call Rick back.

Chapter Eight

Cari loved new paint. Something about opening the can and seeing the creamy mix brought her comfort. It represented home and work and creativity, all things she craved and wanted. Once she had these walls painted, she'd refurbish the wainscoting and the window seals and borders. She wanted to scrape away all the layers to get to the real wood underneath, the heart of the house. Same with the staircase. Somewhere underneath the aged off-white paint, there was real mahogany. She remembered it that way and she did have a few pictures from her childhood.

Her contractor, a fatherly man named Rod Green, was just as excited about the renovations as she was. He knew Victorian houses;

he'd been working with several other families in Knotwood Mountain to keep their homes intact.

Why hadn't Doreen done the same with this house? It was built around the turn of the century and it was still so beautiful, even now with the last of the sun setting out the front bay windows. Cari would never understand why Doreen had insisted they move from this house in the first place. And Cari had hated the modern cedar house out on the river, even if the surroundings were tranquil and the views stunning.

Or maybe she'd just hated being uprooted and plopped back down in the midst of strangers, her own father changing overnight from loving and concerned to distant and uncaring. Doreen had certainly done a number on him.

Putting those bad memories aside, Cari concentrated instead on the future ahead. The green she'd tested on one small corner of the big wall looked great in the muted light of dusk. She hoped it would be pretty in the early-morning light, too.

Because her budget was tight and the old walls held coats of plain white, she hadn't put on a primer, but she had sanded the rough spots until the old walls looked smooth and ready to get a quick face-lift. Now she'd managed to cover half of one entire wall with the rich green. She stood back and sipped water and nibbled cheese puffs from an open bag, admiring the way the color had cheered up this big open room. It wasn't a major redo but it did make her feel as if she'd accomplished something important.

She was about to get back to painting when someone knocked on the door.

"I need to get a bell," she murmured. She'd had more visitors this week than she'd had in a month back in Atlanta.

For a small town, Knotwood Mountain always had something going on and, with high tourist season beginning, the foot traffic out on the street was picking up. She could hear soulful jazz music coming from the square up by the river park. And every now and then, she'd hear laughter echoing from the river as a group of rafters floated by.

But when she got to the door and saw the man standing underneath the porch light, her heart tripped and sputtered to a stop. All she could hear was the pumping of her pulse inside her head.

Rick Adams.

She hadn't called him about dinner. But apparently, that didn't matter now.

When he knocked again, she called out, "Just a minute." She couldn't hide since he'd probably seen her through the window. Glancing at herself in an old, pockmarked mirror by the door, she groaned. "No makeup and lots of paint smears." And she was wearing cutoff jean shorts, an old UGA T-shirt and her purple fuzzy slippers. Oh, well.

"Cari? I know you're home. And I promised you dinner. So let me in, okay?"

She opened the door, careful to keep the chain lock on. "Rick, I'm not prepared for company. I—"

"But I brought dinner," he said. "Pizza from the Pizza Haus—you remember it? The one that sits right on the river? We all used to hang out there after school and weekends. I ordered the house special, loaded with all that bad stuff that's so good."

Oh, this was so not fair. Had Jolena also told him about Cari's penchant for junk food? A penchant that had once caused her to put on too many pounds?

Her godmother was even more conniving than she'd realized. In a good way, of course, but still…

He knocked again, softly. "Cari, Jolena is worried about you. I offered to come and check on you."

She gave in and yanked the door open, staring up at him in disbelief. "Jolena forced you to come and check on me?"

"No, not exactly. Technically I offered, since, technically I wanted to take you to dinner tonight. I'll have to practice my powers of persuasion a little more. They don't seem to work on you."

"I'll just reckon…." She groaned as the distinctive smell of deep-dish pizza lifted out to her nose. "I'm not dressed for company."

"You look adorable," he said, shoving his way toward the kitchen. "Oh, you got my flowers. I love the slippers, by the way."

She looked down at her feet. She'd already forgotten about her purple feathery slippers with sequins sprinkled across the feathers— just one of the many feminine items she'd carried in her shop in Atlanta.

Nothing to do about that now, however. "Thanks for the flowers and the pizza, but I didn't say you could come in."

"You didn't slam the door in my face either."

He took a slice of pizza out of the white

box and moved it in front of her nose. "Jolena said you don't eat right."

"I wouldn't call *that* eating right," she replied, pointing to the tempting veggie pizza. "Maybe the veggies, but certainly not the crust."

"She said you skipped lunch today. You need to eat."

"I used to eat, a lot," she said, her resolve dissolving against his endearing smile. "I used food and shopping to make up for my lack of having a family, but I don't want to go back to my old habits." With food or with the wrong man, she reminded herself.

He wasn't buying that excuse. "There's a big difference between eating to survive and stay healthy and starving yourself out of fear."

That made her mad. "So you think I'm starving myself? Out of fear? What kind of fear? Did Jolena also tell you that?"

He put down the pizza slice and crossed his arms, clearly here for the long haul. "She didn't have to. I figured that one out all on my own. Stress does that to a person. You're afraid you'll get fat. Aren't most women afraid of that? It doesn't mean you have to dry up and waste away. And I've watched enough reality television to know it's not about the food. You said it yourself. You were craving something else."

She tried to be flippant in the face of his armchair analysis. "And you would know this because?"

"Because I've been there myself, you know, trying to please everyone else. Trying to live up to a certain expected image, trying to find atonement. But sometimes, you just have to let go and have a pizza-fest, darlin'."

Cari wanted to tell him to leave and take his pizza with him, but something in his eyes, the same something she'd caught a glimpse of when they'd first reconnected, tugged at her. "So…you couldn't find a date tonight either?"

"I had a date—with you. I wanted to take a very stubborn new-girl-back-in-town out to a fancy dinner, but she refused to allow me that luxury. So here I am, bearing one of your favorite meals out of sheer desperation."

"You've never been desperate a day in your life," she said as she grabbed a wipe rag. "C'mon. I'll find us something to drink. And if you're nice, I might let you help me finish painting that wall over there." Stopping to wash her hands in the old sink, she looked at him over her shoulder. "There's an action movie coming on television later. I guess you could stay and watch that with me, too."

"Deal." He grabbed the pizza and followed her back to the living room.

She motioned toward the window seat where the bay window looked out over the street then went to her new refrigerator to get two soft drinks. When she came back, he had the pizza box open and waiting, his smile triumphant. "So you like action movies?"

Out on the sidewalk, someone walked by, headed to one of the nearby nightspots on the river, their talk and laughter spilling through the open windows of the old house.

"Yes, I do. It's my little secret. I guess it helps me to blow off steam without actually doing harm."

"I've never known such a girly-girl to like manly movies with shoot-'em-ups and car chases. It's kinda cute, in a very scary way."

Cari didn't know how to explain. "It started after my mother died. I'd spend hours in my room upstairs, watching movies. Sometimes, that was the only thing on and so I got hooked. Of course, we moved out of this house pretty quickly when things changed."

He gave her a sympathetic look. "You mean when Doreen took over."

She nodded, sipped her drink. "Yes. Her idea of family was a bit overblown for my tastes. Doreen always wanted to invite prominent people over for a sit-down dinner, which usually meant I'd be in the kitchen washing up dishes while everyone else was having dessert. She is so not like my mother. My mother knew how to make things perfect. She was a polite, kind woman. I miss that."

"I'm sorry," he said, his eyes holding hers. "I miss my dad. We went through some strained times before he died and I wish we'd had time to really get to know each other. But I have my mom and my brother, Simon. I'll take you out to the ranch to meet him sometime. He'd like you. And I can get you a good deal on a pair of handmade boots."

She liked the way his laugh lines crinkled when he smiled. "You're blessed to be close to both of them. Me, I had this nice little family, in this perfect old Victorian house. But that went away the day my mother died. I think my dad and I could have worked through things if Doreen hadn't come along. That's what I regret the most, that we didn't get a chance to just grieve together and grow stronger by helping each other."

"So you're still rebelling by indulging in action movies now and then?"

"Something like that. But I really do enjoy them."

He grinned and grabbed another slice. Glancing over at the wall, he said, "That looks good. I'll help you finish it so we can get to the movie."

She almost told him, no, never mind. She was supposed to be miffed with him after all. But painting with a buddy was a lot more fun than painting alone. Still, she wanted to offer him a way out. "I was just teasing. You don't have to paint, since you brought dinner."

"I'm here and I want to help," Rick countered. "Can you just let me do that, please?"

He sounded sincere. But she had to torment him a little. "Did Bridget stand you up or something?"

He put down his drink. "I was wondering when we'd get around to that subject." Shrugging, he said, "Look, Bridget is a mixed-up woman who's lonely and confused."

"Oh, I thought that was me."

"You might be mixed up right now, but

your heart is in the right place. I can see that. I'm not even sure Bridget has a heart."

She couldn't help but smile at that. "But Bridget seems to think you two have something going on. She sure tried to give me that impression."

"She's wrong." He chewed a piece of crust then leaned forward. "But it's nice to see that you might be a tad jealous. That means you like me a little bit."

Cari threw down her pizza. "This is not jealousy. It's more like shock. Seeing you so friendly with her really threw me, but I don't have any right to be thrown. Let's just drop it, okay."

He studied her face. "I tried to make it up to you."

"Oh, you mean with flowers and food. That usually does the trick for me. So I'd say you've done enough."

"And painting, don't forget that. I am a Picasso with a paintbrush."

She giggled at that. And in spite of her worries, this man did make her laugh. She liked that. A lot.

When he kept watching her, she started to feel self conscious. "What?"

He pushed a napkin toward her cheek. "You

have pizza sauce, right there by that lovely mint-green paint smudge." He gently wiped at her face. "There, all gone—the pizza, that is. The paint seems to be dried on good."

Cari had to swallow to hide all the crazy emotions tripping over themselves inside her heart. Fear? She certainly had that. Hope? It was trying to creep back into her soul. Trust? Wasn't so sure about that one yet. But just the brush of the crumpled napkin against her skin made her go all soft and mushy inside.

It had been a very long time since anyone had pampered her or tried to help her. Telling herself she was too needy, taking pleasure in junk food and a man who didn't even know her pain or her flaws, she let the moment slip by. And reminded herself that Rick Adams had his own agenda, flowers and pizza and neediness aside. And she'd be wise to remember that.

Rick couldn't get this moment out of his mind. His hand holding the stiff white paper napkin against her skin. Her eyes going all wild and wide while she looked at him like a trapped animal needing tender loving care. He'd seen it all there in her eyes, the fear, the need, the distrust and the hope. And he'd felt her pain as clearly as if it had been his own, because he understood her pain so clearly—maybe because it *had* been his own. How to make her see that?

By allowing her to get used to you, came the answer. He couldn't push this, no matter the erratic feelings surging together like river currents inside his soul, and no matter the outcome. He had to give Cari time to adjust, time to realize he wasn't the same person she remembered from high school—even if he did talk to leggy blondes on occasion.

"Let's do some painting," he said, tossing the napkin on the coffee table.

She gave him another confused glance. "Are you sure? I mean, you don't have to babysit me. I'm okay, really. I don't mind spending a Friday night alone. Sometimes, I just need to get away and think, have some quiet time."

"So you want me to leave now, after telling me I could stay, after eating my pizza?"

"No, no, I'm not saying that. I don't want you to feel obligated to stay out of pity."

Rick's heart did a strange little jump. This was different. This was innocent and unassuming and wonderful. This woman didn't care about his status or his bank account, not like the women he'd dated in Atlanta. She only wanted to make sure he wasn't sitting here with her out of some sense of obligation.

If only she knew. He couldn't leave her now, not if his life depended on it. "I want to be here, Cari," he finally said. "And it has nothing to do with feeling sorry for you, okay?"

"Then why did you come?" she asked, clearly shocked.

Which simply endeared her to him even more. "I wanted to see you again," he replied. "That's all."

"But what about—"

He put a finger to her lips. "Not tonight. Tonight let's just enjoy getting to know each other and forget about all the other stuff. Let's paint that wall."

She didn't argue anymore. Instead she got up and found him a paintbrush. For a while, they worked in comfortable silence, the swish, swish of their brushes finding a rhythm that made a nice melody. Then he heard the crunch of cheesy puffs and he looked over to see her wiping cheese powder off her face.

"Here." She offered him the bag. He helped her finish it off.

Finally, Rick asked, "Did you ever think we'd both wind up back here in Knotwood Mountain?"

She stopped painting. "I never wanted to leave, except to go to college. That was my parents' hope for me, so I wanted to get an education then come back here. I've never told anyone this, but I always had a dream of running my little shop right here on First Street. I just never expected to take so many detours to get back here. And I never imagined I'd lose my parents before I saw my dream come true. Or that my little shop would be right here in this house."

He shook his head. "Ironic, huh? I couldn't wait to get away from here. I thought Atlanta was the place where I'd find my fortune and settle down. I found the fortune, but the settling down part didn't go so great." He shrugged. "I wanted certain things—a home and family. And she wanted certain things I couldn't give her—status and a social standing. We parted ways when I realized she wasn't going to marry me because she didn't think I had enough of the 'it' factor. And I'm still not sure what 'it' is."

"Oh, I think you have *it*," Cari said, laughing. "And bless her heart, it sounds as if she won't be happy with anyone."

"Good point."

Cari dipped her roller then brought it back to the wall. "I had such a crush on you back in high school."

He turned to stare at her. She had paint on her cheek and in her hair. She looked embarrassed. "You did? Why didn't you ever clue me in on that?"

"Yeah, like you would have noticed. You had a girlfriend remember? What was her name? Ginger Cunningham?"

Rick nodded. "Good ol' Ginger. She's married now with three children. Married a farmer. Go figure."

Cari didn't say anything. "You had lots of girlfriends, if I remember correctly."

Rick wondered if he'd done something to hurt her way back then—back when he was so shallow and such a jerk. "I wish we'd been friends in school. I mean that."

She laughed. "No you don't. We can be friends now because we've both changed a lot. But you and me in high school—like oil and water. It's the same old clichéd story. You were the big man on campus. I was a few years behind you—a sophomore when you were a senior—the wallflower who rarely went to any of the fun events. And in the two years after my mother's death, I gained about twenty pounds and became a really bitter person. So no, we couldn't be friends."

He looked sheepish and felt lower than a snake's belly. "I didn't recognize you the other day when you were looking at the red shoes."

She wasn't buying it. "No, you didn't even *remember* me. But that's okay. I wasn't very memorable back then."

He lifted his head to stare at her, trying to convey complete honesty. "Well, you certainly are now."

She looked doubtful, but she nodded again. "Let's finish up and watch the movie."

"Good." After they'd washed their brushes and rollers from the old spigot on the back porch, Rick kicked off his loafers and settled down beside her on the floor.

Using the love seat and fat cushions as a headrest, they sat on the floor in front of the tiny television.

So far so good, he decided, determined to remember everything about her and this night. "Nothing like a good car chase to take your mind off the reality of life."

"That's what I always say," she replied with a grin.

Then she put her feet out in front of her and kicked off her feathery slippers, grinning at Rick with the sweet enticement that seemed to surround her when she was happy.

And right now, this very minute, she seemed very happy.

I'm in serious trouble, he thought. Serious.

But he couldn't stop smiling.

"By the way, really, thank you for the flowers," she murmured as the intro to the movie began. "I love them."

"You're welcome."

He smiled over at her then turned toward the television. And accepted the way all of his protective instincts seemed to merge together while he watched her watching the movie.

Having a spoiled lonely blonde chasing him was interesting and flattering—that was one thing. But to be floored by a sprite of a woman who wore feathered, sequined slippers, ate cheesy puffs and painted walls green was quite another.

Rick felt as if his boring, normal life had just become every bit as exciting as an action movie. And he had a feeling he was in for the ride of his life.

Chapter Nine

Cari woke up and rolled over to find pink and orange ribbons of sunrise lifting out across the mountains.

Glancing around, she stretched and remembered Rick had been here last night, eating pizza, painting and watching a movie with her. They'd talked a bit, laughed some, finished off their food then settled back. Somewhere in there, he'd reached for her hand. About halfway through the good guys chasing the bad guys, she'd gotten drowsy.

She must have drifted off, because next thing she knew, he was nudging her off his shoulder, telling her the movie was over.

"Hey, Sleeping Beauty. Time for me to get home. Go on up to bed and I'll make sure everything's locked up down here."

Cari had nodded, mumbled good-night and quickly went up, washed her face and brushed her teeth then climbed into her bed. And she'd slept like a baby for the first time in weeks.

Because of Rick. He made her feel safe.

She got up and stretched, then got ready for her day. She needed coffee. Padding down the old stairs in her bare feet, she glanced around and saw a note taped to the flower vase. Practically skipping, Cari ran to read it.

"You fell asleep and missed the best part. The good guys won. They always do. I'll call you later. Rick."

Cari held the note in her hands, wondering what was happening to her. Was he one of the good guys? He sure seemed that way. He was a gentleman, kind and chivalrous. He was a shrewd businessman, self-confident and sure. And he was a charmer, no doubt about that. She imagined he helped little old ladies across the street and took in stray animals, too. Definitely hero material.

Not that she was looking.

"What have I done?" she asked as the coffee machine timer kicked on and the dark brew started pouring into the carafe. "What have I done?"

She should have stopped him at the door last night. But instead, she'd let him come in, bearing food and charm, and sit with her, talk to her, laugh with her. And make her feel special. He'd allowed her to fall asleep holding his hand.

"I'm in trouble," she said. And she needed to think about this, a lot more. First, church, lunch with Jolena's family then a Sunday afternoon of painting the rest of the downstairs. That would require a lot of fortitude. And take her mind off Rick, she hoped.

The phone rang, jarring her out of her worries.

Cari saw the caller ID then clicked on the receiver. "Jolena, you are so busted."

"Hush and tell me everything. Did he come by? Did you go out to dinner? Where did you go?"

"Hold on," Cari replied, groaning. "I haven't even had my coffee yet."

"Hurry up. You gotta get ready for church."

"I'll be at church but I just woke up." Cari sighed, inhaled about half a cup of black coffee then cleared her throat. "He came by, thanks to you. And he brought dinner with him."

"Pizza?"

"Yes, since you also told him about that, too. I ate two slices. Thanks very much."

"It won't kill you to indulge now and then."

"I'll have to work it off. I'll have to work off a lot of things."

"So did you two talk? What happened?"

"We talked a bit but he didn't want to discuss any issues or leggy blondes, although he did say he doesn't care about Bridget in that way. He helped me paint a wall and he watched my action movie with me."

"You and those movies, I declare." Jolena's laugh bubbled over the phone. "And then?"

"And then I fell asleep sitting up straight, leaning against the couch—well, actually I think I leaned against his shoulder, too. He woke me and told me he'd let himself out and lock the door for me. I went to bed and fell into a deep stupor. I woke up and found a note on the flowers. He's going to call me later."

"It's a good start. A very good start."

"You know this can't go anywhere, don't you?"

"And why not? And girl, I'm not just talking merger in the sense of a *business* merger. I'm talking merger between two of the cutest people I've ever laid eyes on. You two belong together."

"And how can you know that?"

"I know things, is all," Jolena replied. "Now get on with yourself and get dressed. I'll see you at church. Then we'll go to brunch at my mama's house."

"I can't overeat," Cari said. "But I can't resist your mother's cooking, either."

"Oh, oh. We'll talk at church. Meet me at the doughnut stand in the fellowship hall."

"I'll be there, but no doughnuts for me."

Cari hung up, smiled at Jolena's antics then stared at the flowers bursting forth in front of her eyes.

"This can't happen," she said as she touched one of the fat, lush lilies. "It can't. It's just not possible."

She should make a list of all the reasons why hanging out with Rick Adams wasn't possible, but right now she just wanted more coffee and more time to savor how much she'd enjoyed having him here last night.

"It was worth the extra calories and fat," she decided as she headed toward the bathroom. "And so worth giving up some of my wounded pride."

But taking things further wouldn't be worth the risk of losing her heart, she decided.

Somehow, she'd have to make him see that.

It didn't help that he was sitting front and center at church and wearing a nice white shirt and a pretty red striped tie. And spiffy black cowboy boots.

It didn't help that she'd dressed extra carefully in a full-skirted vintage green dress she'd found at an antique shop in Conyers, Georgia, or that she'd fluffed her hair and put on mascara and perfume.

And it really didn't help when he turned and caught her looking at him, his smile sure and easy. When he motioned for her to come and sit by him and his mother, she just smiled and shook her head. She needed to stay back in the pew with Jolena. Just so she could take it all in.

As they stood to sing the opening hymn, Cari looked around the old country church. It had been here for over a century and was well maintained and pristine, its walls a pretty stained pine and its high ceiling arched over solid wooden beams. The stained-glass windows glinted like jewels in the sunlight and the old pews felt polished and warm to her touch. Being here renewed her spirit and her commitment to make things work this time around.

I need You, Lord. I need You in my corner.

He had always been there, she knew. But Cari hadn't always turned to God in times of stress or even in times of blessings. She turned to Him now, secure that He would help her through this transition. And maybe, just maybe, He'd help her learn to forgive and forget, too.

When the service was over, her good mood went south, however. Doreen was going out the door ahead of her, wearing a pink silk dress and bone-colored pumps and smiling up at the minister. "Such a good sermon, Reverend. We could all certainly learn a thing or two about humility around here, don't you think?" She turned and shot Cari a knowing glance then kept moving.

Cari said hello to the minister and caught the sense of disapproval he gave her even while he smiled and welcomed her back. Doreen had struck again with just a word whispered, no doubt.

Cari held up her head and kept moving, the

bright sunshine making her squint. When a hand touched her arm, she whirled to find Doreen standing there.

"Good morning," Cari said, trying to move away.

"Hold on," Doreen replied. "I need to have a word with you."

Cari braced herself, wondering what she'd done now. "All right."

"Bridget said she ran into you the other day and you were downright hostile toward her."

Cari had to smile. "We did see each other, but I don't recall—"

Doreen raised a hand. "You listen to me, missy. You might think you can come here and be Miss High-and-Mighty just because you're a Duncan, but that isn't going to change the way people around here view you. We all know the truth. You stayed away when your poor father was deathly ill, while I nursed him and tried to take care of both him and his business. Now you march back in and start trying to take over the town, getting other people to do your dirty work. It won't work, Cari. You'll fail like you always have." She finished in a flurry of breaths. "And another thing, stay away from

Brady. I don't need the likes of you influencing my son."

Cari stood there with her mouth open, so shocked she couldn't breathe. "I came home as soon as I heard Daddy was sick. You didn't let me know until it was almost too late." She inhaled and swallowed the lump in her throat. "And I care about Brady. You should know that."

"I only know I don't want you around my children."

Cari lifted her chin. "I won't bother Brady and I certainly don't intend to get chummy with Bridget."

Doreen looked smug. "That's because you can't compete with her. Even if rumor has it you've been buttering up to Rick Adams. You don't stand a chance."

With that, Doreen turned and pranced to her Mercedes.

And Cari stood there, face blazing, while half the town looked on.

Rick hurried over and grabbed Cari by the arm. "Let's get out of here."

She stood frozen, resisting him. "Let me go."

"No, I won't let you go. And I've got a

good mind to go after that woman and tell her exactly what I think about her *commands* to you. She's not your boss, Cari. She's not even related to you."

"Thank goodness," Cari said, looking down at the ground. "But I don't want you running interference with Doreen. She'd make your life miserable, too. I just want her to leave me alone."

"You can't let her get to you." He urged her toward his Jeep. "A lot of people in this town have her number and I think you'd be surprised how many of them are glad you're back."

"I doubt that. The minister could barely look me in the eye. She has him in her pocket so why should I expect any better from everyone else?"

"You can expect better from me. Remember that."

"I need to get out of here."

"I'll drive you home."

She held back, the old wall of shame clearly falling around her again. "I'm supposed to go to Jolena's for Sunday brunch. She'll be worried."

He glanced around and spotted Jolena shooing her four daughters toward the car. "Let's go talk to her."

Jolena took one look at Cari's face and grabbed her by the hands. "What on earth?"

"Doreen ambushed her," Rick said, gritting his teeth. Only his mother holding him back had kept him from telling Doreen Duncan what she could do with her superior attitude. The nerve of that woman. "I'm taking her home."

"Why don't you bring her on to Mama's house," Jolena suggested. "And your mama, too. We always have plenty for everybody."

He looked at Cari. "Would you like that?"

She still looked shell-shocked, but she nodded. "Just get me out of here, please."

An hour later, Rick sat with Cari at a picnic table out underneath an ancient live oak in Mildred Bell's big backyard. The old farmhouse sat whitewashed and looming, right in the middle of a big pasture with mountain vistas all around. A round white gazebo covered with a lush morning glory vine stood, looking like a wedding cake, out near a little pond just past the yard.

"Nice place," he said. "Eat your food."

Cari refused to look at him. "I'm not very hungry."

She'd been quiet on the ride out here. Thankfully, everyone had left her alone.

Jolena and his mother had retreated into the kitchen with all the others, intent on getting the potluck dinner set out so the carloads of family and friends could eat.

Trying to make her laugh, he said, "I've never seen a brunch quite like this one. Roast beef and gravy, rice and potatoes, fresh tomatoes and corn, pound cake and coconut cake. I'll have to hang with Jolena and her mom more often."

"They have a large, loving family."

And she didn't.

No wonder she was so close to Jolena.

"So you've known them all a long time?"

"Since I was a baby. Jolena used to work with my mother at the food bank and when I was born, my parents asked her to be my god-mother. She'd babysit me every now and then when they traveled. They had been friends since they were little. My mother's family owned the neighboring farm, but they sold out a long time ago. She was the only one left. And now, I guess I'm the only one."

He finally gave up trying to get her to eat. Taking her hands in his, he said, "But you're not alone, Cari. You know that, don't you?"

She finally looked up at him, her eyes full of a misty misery. "I am alone. I've been alone since my father married Doreen and turned away from me. But I'm used to it. And I need to remember that."

She got up to leave, but he held her back, his hand clutching hers. "Don't be like this. You came back to change all of that. You can't let Doreen's bitterness discourage you. You're better than that."

"Am I?" She whirled on him then, the anger in her eyes like lightning, quick and full of fury. "I came back to find a way to make that woman pay. That's why I really came back. And somehow, I'm going to make her suffer the same way she made me suffer. I won't be humiliated by her again. Ever."

With that, she walked toward the gazebo, her green skirt flaring out around her legs, her head held high. But he watched as she reached up to wipe the tears off her face.

Rick had never seen such anger, such pain. It tore at him, making him realize he'd only thought he knew suffering and despair. But he'd always had a loving family to support him, even when he'd strayed or made big mistakes. And thankfully, he and his father had mended some of their differences long before his father passed away.

What would it be like to become an outcast? To lose a mother to death and a father to another family?

"Everything okay, son?"

He turned to find his mother staring at him with worry in her eyes.

"No, it's not okay. But I hope I can make it better. She just needs a friend, someone to show her how to let go of all that resentment."

"Careful," Gayle warned. "If she's not ready to let go, you might get caught in the cross fire."

"I'm already caught," he admitted. "I can't turn my back on her now."

Gayle shook her head. "This is messy stuff. Doreen won't go down without a fight."

Rick nodded. "You've always told me life can get messy. I just have to deal with it."

Gayle touched a hand to his arm. "Then go out there and talk to her. I'm going to help clean up and catch a ride home with Jolena."

"Thanks, Mom."

"Call me later," she said with a smile.

Rick waved to her then started walking toward the gazebo, his focus on Cari.

She was sitting there, gazing out over the pond, her back to him. And it struck him once again that she looked like a princess trapped in a tower. She was all tangled up in grief and bitterness and so very lost.

She was a princess who really did need to be rescued. From herself.

He just hoped he could be the one to help her, if she'd let him.

Chapter Ten

Rick took Cari back to the church to get her car. Hopping out of the Jeep, he came around to help her down. "Are you gonna be all right?"

She gave him a crooked smile. "I'll be fine. I expected this so I just have to deal with it. She caught me off guard this morning, but this is nothing new, really. Every time I called to speak to my father, every time I tried to send him birthday or Christmas gifts, I was met with this kind of hostility, and my father heard only what Doreen wanted him to hear, I'm sure. Bridget obviously gave her mother a different version of our meeting, coloring me in a bad light, of course. But I can't let it sidetrack me. I just need to keep my nose to the grindstone and stay focused."

"Now you're talking." He wanted to hug her close, to shield her from any more pain but Cari wasn't the kind of girl to fall into a man's arms easily. She was like a wounded bird. She needed a bit of coaxing.

"I'd better go," she said. "I've got lots to do today."

"I could come and help."

"No." She shook her head. "I just need some time alone."

"All right." He pulled a card out of his wallet. "My cell number is on there. Call me if you need me. I'm usually out at my ranch on weekends."

"You mentioned that. I'd like to see it sometime if the offer is still there."

Glad to change the subject, he nodded. "You have an open invitation. It's a few miles north of town near the river. I have horses, if you'd like to ride."

"That might be nice." She glanced away. "I'm glad it's not near Doreen's house." Her father's second wife lived south of town. Not far enough away but good, all the same.

"Maybe next weekend," Rick said.

"Maybe." She didn't sound too excited. "I'd like that."

He took her hand in his, staring down at

their joined fingers. Rubbing his other hand across her knuckles, he said, "I'll see you later, then. And I'll follow you back into town."

She put a hand on her car door then stopped. "You go ahead. I need to visit my parents' grave site."

Not wanting to intrude, Rick had no choice but to get in the Jeep and leave. But he stopped at the end of the lane and looked off to the right where the old cemetery lay underneath an outcropping of hills and rocks. His father was buried in that cemetery and he often went to visit the grave site. He understood Cari's need for solitude and privacy but he didn't want to leave her here alone.

The cemetery was well tended and beautiful. Old live oaks formed canopies on each corner of the big lot and crape myrtle and magnolia trees lined the many paths. Stone benches were set here and there, offering rest to the weary and heartbroken. The wind moaned like a sob across the hills and valleys, its song at once soothing and solemn.

Cari walked toward an elaborate memorial stone placed near a towering magnolia tree. She stood for a minute then sank down to her knees, her hands going to her face, her shoulders shaking.

Rick sat there, torn between going to her and giving her some space. He couldn't leave. He turned the Jeep around so he was facing the cemetery and he pulled off the lane and shut down the motor. Then before he could talk himself out of it, he got out of the Jeep and hurried to her.

"Cari?" He sank down beside her. "Cari, I'm here."

She turned to gaze at him, her eyes misty and full of tears. Rick took one look at her face then gathered her into his arms and let her cry.

After a while, she pulled back to wipe at her face then looked down at the two graves. "We had such plans, my mom and I. She was going to take my best friend Tiffany and me on a trip to Europe after we graduated from high school. We started planning it my freshman year." She shrugged and let out a shuddering sob. "She died my sophomore year. And then everything changed. I lost both of them that year. My father just shut down."

Rick swallowed the lump in his throat. "It must have been so hard, dealing with all of that and trying to go to school, too." He wished he'd gone on instincts back then and reached out to her. Well, he was here now and he wasn't about to give up on her.

She nodded, wiped at her eyes again. "I wish we'd had some time alone, you know? I think we could have grown closer. But Doreen didn't allow us that time. She went after him with a vengeance. And she won. She always wins."

Rick didn't know how to help her get past this, so he held her close, hoping his physical presence would be enough for now. And he said a silent prayer, asking God to heal her and ease her pain.

He stayed with her until she got up, then he held her hand as they walked back to her car. She smiled up at him, her lips trembling. "Thank you."

He didn't ask if she'd be okay. He just leaned close and wiped at her damp cheek. "I'll check on you later." Only after he'd watched her drive away did he get back in the Jeep and leave.

And he watched her car through the rearview mirror until she turned off toward town.

Cari had seen Rick's Jeep parked up near the road.

He'd waited for her and then he'd come to

her. He was that kind of man, the kind who stayed, the kind who listened and didn't ask questions. The kind of man she'd always dreamed of finding. Maybe she'd been waiting to return here to Rick all this time.

But that scene with Doreen this morning had brought all her old hurts and insecurities back to the surface. Which meant she had no business dreaming about a relationship with any man right now, let alone a man that Bridget had her eyes on. Even if Rick wasn't interested, Bridget would be territorial and demanding and she'd paint an ugly picture regarding Cari—a picture that some in this town would believe, no matter the truth.

Pulling her car up to the small garage behind the house, Cari wondered if she'd have the strength to finish what she'd started. Had she been wrong to come home?

Maybe Doreen was right. Maybe she should put a For Sale sign on the old house and get out while she still had a chance.

But you just promised your parents you wouldn't do that.

Did they hear me, Lord? Does anyone up there hear me?

She prayed so. She had a few weeks until

the big Fourth of July weekend and the crush of tourists who'd pass along these streets. She needed to start setting up her boutique. And that meant putting all of this out of her mind and at least getting the downstairs ready for business.

The paperwork and business permits were in place and she had the loan from the bank. The rest of her inventory was stored at a warehouse in Atlanta, just waiting to be shipped. And once she set up her computer system, she could order more stock online and get back to working on her own designs, too.

She had a perfect room upstairs to use as a workshop but for now, she could work out of the kitchen if she had to. Feeling better now that she'd had a chance to get back on track, she hurried up the back steps.

And saw that the back door was standing wide open.

Calling out, Cari stepped inside. "Who's there?"

No answer. But she didn't need anyone to shout out why her door was ajar.

She saw the reason right there on the walls. The newly painted walls.

Someone had broken in here and left her a message.

"Go back to Atlanta, loser."

The ugly message, along with a few other choice words, was sprawled in heavy black lettering across the big wall she and Rick had just finished painting. And the rest of her precious green paint was now splattered across the old hardwood floors and all over what little furniture she'd put out.

So much for being determined.

So much for trying to save money by doing some of this work herself. She'd have to get the contractor in immediately to restore the floors.

Cari didn't think she had any tears left to cry after pouring out her heart at the cemetery. So she didn't cry. She just stood there staring, wondering who in the world would break into her house on a beautiful Sunday morning and do this.

Then it hit her and she felt sick to her stomach.

Had this been a random act, teenagers out for a good time?

Or had Doreen and Bridget set out to leave her a definite message?

Rick reached down to pet the golden retriever he'd adopted from the pound three years ago. "How you doing, Shiloh? Have you been a good boy for Uncle Simon?"

Shiloh danced around his master, his big tongue wagging right along with his fluffy tail.

The door to the big cabin opened and Rick's older brother walked out to stand on the porch. "I'm not that dog's uncle. Now if you want to get married and have some babies, I'll be glad to claim them as my kin."

Rick laughed out loud, used to Simon's bluster. "You love Shiloh and you know it."

"No, I don't." But even as he denied it, Simon whistled to the big dog. Shiloh came running to take one of the treats Simon always kept in his pocket. "What're you doing out here so late on a Sunday anyway?"

Rick wondered that himself. "I didn't feel like going back to my usual Sunday afternoon paperwork. I think I'll go for a nice long ride on Pepper. I'm sure he could use the exercise."

"Uh-huh." Simon settled down on the steps then stared up at his brother, his dark eyes alert and all-knowing. "You must have something heavy weighing on your mind. Nothing ever keeps you away from that store."

Rick took in his brother's old jeans and

faded T-shirt. And the boots. It figured that the world-famous boot maker wouldn't bother to make himself a decent pair of shoes. Simon's brown work boots were scuffed and well-worn, but they were still together. A testament to his brother's amazing talent since this had been one of the first pairs he'd ever designed. "You think?"

"I know. You always work. You only come out here and put that stallion through his paces whenever you're fretting over something. Or someone. What's her name?"

"Who said it had anything to do with a woman?"

Simon grinned, his eyes as dark and rich as the river. "Doesn't it always?"

"How would you know? You haven't left this ranch since—"

Simon stopped grinning. "We weren't talking about me."

"Sorry." Rick wanted to kick himself. Simon had lost his wife to cancer when they'd only been married five years. And in the five years since, his brother had become even more of a recluse. Wondering how anyone recovered from that kind of grief, Rick sat down beside Simon and pulled Shiloh close to pet him. "I didn't mean to remind you."

"I'm reminded every day, brother. Let's get back to you."

Rick looked out toward the bluff where the Chattahoochee ran through their property. "Do you remember Cari Duncan? Carinna Duncan?"

Simon squinted. "I know the name, of course."

"She was James and Natalie Duncan's only child."

Simon nodded. "But the old man remarried, right? Some redhead?"

"Yep. A redhead with two children of her own."

"Okay. What's this got to do with you?"

"Cari's back in Knotwood Mountain and she's moved into the old Duncan House, right by our store."

Simon shook his head then looked at Rick. "And you just happen to have noticed this, right?"

Rick inhaled then sputtered out a breath. "Oh, yeah. In fact, I cosigned on a loan for her at the bank. Mom thinks I've lost some marbles."

"And while I don't always agree with our mother, I have to say she might be right on this one. What were you thinking?"

Rick wondered that himself. "I was thinking about helping someone who needed a friend. Cari's solid, Simon. She has a good plan to renovate the place and turn it from an eyesore to a showcase. I'm just a silent investor, her insurance policy."

Simon sat up to stare out into the trees. "You know I don't want any part of running that store, but did it ever occur to you to ask Mom and me about this before you went headlong into it?"

"Well, yes, it did occur to me. But as you just stated, you've pretty much left the business end of things up to me. And Mom never approves of any of the girls I've dated so I thought I'd try something different."

"I'll say. Sure is a risky way to get to a woman's heart. What if she defaults on this loan?"

"Then Jolena Beasley and I will have a nice piece of downtown property to hold and develop or sell for a profit. But she won't default. I know she won't."

Simon got up and brushed off his jeans, his cynical nature evident in his scowl. "You need to get on that horse and go for a good ride, Rick. And clear you head. I can't believe you. I just can't."

Rick got up, too. "I don't need you to believe me. It's a done deal. And I have faith in Cari and her abilities. Even if some people around here don't."

"How well do you know this woman?"

"I went to high school with her."

Simon slapped a hand to his leg. "Well, then, that makes it right as rain." He gave Rick a hard stare. "When I think of some of the people I knew in high school—well, I sure wouldn't cosign a loan with them, let me tell you."

"Cari's not like that," Rick shot back. "She's gonna make this work. You'll see."

"I'm not the one who needs to be worried," Simon said. "I'm going inside for a sandwich then I'm going back to work. Just in case I have to cover you on this crazy plan."

"You've never had to cover me a day in your life and you know it."

"Well, there's a first time for everything."

Rick watched as his brother went inside, slamming the screen door behind him.

"That went pretty good, didn't it, Shiloh?"

The dog barked a response then waited to see what his master was going to do next. Rick headed for the stables, the dog trotting behind him. He quickly saddled his big white

Arabian stallion. Pepper snorted and whinnied his approval, his white-and-gray mane fluttering around him, while Shiloh waited impatiently, his tail wagging.

"Ornery. That's what my brother is," Rick said, nudging the horse out into the afternoon sun. "Ornery. And lonely. He needs to get out more."

And…maybe I do need to have my head examined.

But Rick didn't think it would come to that. He wasn't worried about Cari's loan. He was worried about Cari's soul. And right now, she was in the battle of her life.

How could he show her that seeking revenge would only destroy her soul and take away her dignity? How could he show her that she had her heart in the right place, coming home? But she had so many wrong reasons for wanting to make her mark in Knotwood Mountain?

Her mind was too wrapped around her pain and anger to see that. She was so caught up in seeking retribution that she might not see what was right in front of her face.

She could make a difference here. She could stand up to the challenge of forgiveness and win.

Or she could fall flat by holding on to her bitterness and this need to get even.

And *that* could cause her to lose everything.

Chapter Eleven

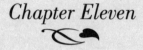

"Sure is a lot going on next door this morning."

Rick turned from thanking a customer who'd just bought a boxed set of mayhaw jam and some fishing gear to see his mother craning her neck at the front window. "What's the matter?"

"Nothing. Looks like Cari's bringing in the big guns. She's got workers coming and going. Guess she's speeding things up so she can open in time for the big Fourth of July weekend."

After calling to make sure Cari was all right last night, Rick had purposely stayed away, hoping to give her some time to regroup. She'd been so down, but this had turned out to be a busy Monday morning in the general store, so he hadn't had a chance to see her. Business was picking up since the fishermen, rafters and campers were coming up for summer vacations. His entire morning had been all about outfitting people with rafts, tubes and tents, not to mention selling a lot of staples such as rice and beans and his mother's famous jellies, jams and nut mixes.

"I know she hopes to get things going over there as soon as possible." He didn't tell his mother that he'd planned to stop by after work to help Cari paint. "Maybe she decided she couldn't get started on her own, after all."

Or maybe she was pouring herself into work to hide her pain. He'd tried that, still fell back on the old routine every now and then.

"Well, since a certain kindly neighbor helped her secure a big loan, I'd think she's got plenty of money to hire all these people anyway."

Rick ignored the pointed quality of his mother's declaration. "Yes, and that's all the more reason to get started." He eyed the clock. "I'm going to Jolena's for the daily special. Want anything?"

Gayle didn't look fooled. "No, I'll get my own when you're back. I've got some spring dresses to put on clearance. And besides, any food you brought back would be cold."

"Oh, and how's that?"

She pursed her lips. "Oh, because knowing you, you'll stop over at Cari's to see how things are progressing, right?"

"Right." She had him there. "I do have a vested interest in the place."

"You can say that again."

He didn't have time for a retort. Several women came in, chattering and laughing and headed upstairs to see what his mom had on clearance. How did women always know when a sale was about to hit?

Rick left before his mother put him to work bringing more clothes out of the stockroom to show these chirpy early birds. He only had one woman on his mind this morning. And he had a nice pair of red pumps on hold for that woman. Come to think of it, he'd put himself on hold for Cari, too. And that was as surprising to him as it would probably be to Cari if he told her that.

Jolena's was packed with the lunch crowd, but he managed to find a stool at the end of the counter. After waving to Jolena, he told the young waitress he'd have the hamburger steak, fresh field peas and dirty rice, with corn bread on the side.

"Want pie with that?" the waitress asked with a toothy grin.

"Of course. How about apple today?"

"Jolena just baked it fresh. And you know how she likes to slice those apples paper thin."

"Oh, then put a scoop of ice cream on top."

Giggling, the girl ran off to get his food.

He was just finishing up the pie when Jolena managed to get a break. "Hey, Rick. How ya doing today?"

"Okay for a hot, crowded Monday. We've been at it all morning. I can smell those tourist dollars."

"Yeah, we've been steady all morning, too." She leaned close. "Have you checked on our girl today?"

"You mean Cari? No. I called her last night, but I've been busy with customers all morning."

"Uh-huh. I talked to her earlier. She's in a fine pickle, let me tell you."

He drained his coffee. "She was upset yesterday, but I made sure she was okay before I left her. I thought she was okay enough last night, even if she didn't talk much. Maybe I should have checked on her in person."

"Then you don't know?"

His pulse went into overdrive. "Know what?"

"Somebody broke into her place while she was at church. Messed things up good. That's why she's got people over there. She's checking into putting in a security system, and well...they're having to redo the floors and—"

"I'm on my way," he said, jumping up to throw the tip on the table. "Put it on my tab."

"Don't I always?"

He didn't answer. "Throw me some corn bread and vegetables into a to-go box. You know she probably hasn't eaten."

Jolena issued orders and soon he had a bag to take to Cari. "Thanks, Jolena."

"Let me know how she's doing."

Rick hurried out of the diner, his goal of staying away from Cari lifting up with the heat waves moving across the asphalt. He couldn't stay away. Cari needed him. She needed his help and his support. Whether she wanted it or not.

Cari sat out on the back porch steps, hot and sweating, her water bottle held to her throbbing head.

It had been a crazy morning but she was

better now. Action meant progress. People milling around meant she was in control.

If only that were true.

"Hi."

She looked up to see Rick standing there, holding a white bag and a big cup full of tea. "Is that from Jolena's?"

"Sure is." He handed her the drink. "Sweet tea with lemon and the vegetable plate with corn bread on the side. And an oatmeal cookie for dessert. And she said to make sure you eat all of it."

Cari took the bag, her mouth watering as the wonderful smells drifted out of the carton. "That won't be a problem. I'm starving."

He sat down beside her. "I had the hamburger steak and gravy with sides. And apple pie."

Her smile was weak. "You are apple pie."

"I'll take that as a compliment."

She didn't say anything for a while. She was too busy breaking her corn bread into the liquid from the creamy peas. Finally, she glanced over at him. "Thank you."

"For what?"

"For looking out for me yesterday after church and calling to check on me last night.

I was a mess. And I don't normally fall apart like that."

"You had good reason."

"Did I? I don't know. I'm going to get through it."

Well, at least she sounded calmer today. Or maybe she was just full of a steely resolve. He still wasn't sure about how to read the many moods of Cari Duncan.

"It's hard, losing a parent. I can't imagine losing both of your parents."

She stared out at the honeysuckle vines. "I just wish I'd told my father I loved him when he could actually comprehend what I was trying to say. I should have insisted Doreen let me visit him more. But I didn't want to upset him when he was so sick—and Doreen indicated that I'd do exactly that so I didn't force the issue. I wish I had, though."

"I'm sure he knew your heart."

"But that's just it. I can't be sure. Doreen poisoned him against me to the point that he didn't trust me at all. That hurts more than anything."

"Well, you need to channel all that hurt into your dreams for Duncan House. Once you get this place back in shape, you'll feel better about things. It'll be a real tribute to your folks."

"If I can keep vandals out so I can accomplish that."

He craned his neck toward the open door. "I heard what happened. Did you report it to the police?"

"Oh, yes. But one of the two available officers told me there's very little they can do about it. He filed a report but he didn't seem that concerned. In fact, he was somewhat bothered that I called him away from his Sunday afternoon nap yesterday."

"Did they check for fingerprints? Ask anyone if they'd seen anything?"

She shook her head. "Most of the businesses on the street were closed when it happened. No one was around. It was over before Jolena's weekend manager opened the diner for the Sunday crowd. Which means whoever did this was probably watching my house, waiting for me to leave."

He didn't like that. "Do you have any ideas?"

She finished off a piece of corn bread. "Oh, yes. But I'll look like the bad guy if I accuse them."

Seeing the anger in her eyes, he said, "You don't think—"

"I know," she replied, pushing her food

away. "I can't prove it, but I know Bridget had something to do with this. And Doreen probably set her up to it. I think they both want me to stay away from Brady. And you."

"I can't believe that." He didn't want to believe that. "It seems so ridiculous."

"Those two will stoop to anything to get me to leave."

"You didn't tell the cops that, did you? It sounds unbelievable. They can't dictate who you talk to or see."

"No, I didn't accuse them. I figured that would be plain stupid. Doreen probably bullies the police around here just as she does everybody else in this town." She gulped down some ice chips. "It's over and I'm calm now. The floors had to be sanded and buffed anyway. Now they just have to remove what was left of my green paint, too. And that wall we did will have to be redone. They didn't take anything, thank goodness, but they left me a very clear message to leave town." She lifted her shoulders. "But I'm not leaving."

Rick admired her stance. She had changed from yesterday. But that scared him. Even though she'd come back from the ledge she seemed to be hovering over yesterday after church, she sounded even more determined today to prove herself. Or to seek revenge.

"Are you sure you're okay?"

"I'm fine. I had my little meltdown and now I've got things in perspective again. Hissy fit number three over and done with." She got up and tossed her garbage in the big trash bin at the end of the alley. "If they want a fight, I'll give them one. But they are not running me out of town. Not this time."

Rick didn't know whether to cheer her on or beg her to think twice. "That's the spirit. Whoever did this was probably just messing around. The place has been empty awhile. I'm sure some of the local kids think it's a good hangout. And now that someone has moved in, they probably don't like it."

"Several people don't like it," she retorted. "Tough."

"Mind if I have a look inside?"

She waved a hand toward the door. "Go ahead. You need to see where all that loan money is going."

He walked through the kitchen, stepping around drop cords, paint buckets and trays and floor sanders. "Looks like the painting is back on track and the floors will look great once they get buffed out."

She looked over the big wide parlor. "Amazing what a few professional painters can get done. I don't know why I didn't just let them do this in the first place."

"What? And miss out on seeing me try to paint a wall?"

She finally laughed. "We did have a lot of paint all over ourselves, didn't we?"

"Yes. But it was fun. We could work on the upstairs while they fix things down here. So you can at least have some privacy up there. Do you have a plan for your living quarters?"

She looked up the narrow staircase. "Oh, yes. A big sitting room, a nice bedroom off the turret room and a major update on the closets and the other bedrooms and baths. And a small efficiency kitchen. I'll keep the big one down here, too."

"Good plan."

Her gaze swept the cluttered room. "I'll never have this ready by the Fourth, no matter how many people Mr. Green brings in."

"If you let me help you, we can make sure you have things up and running in a hurry. You can have your grand opening the weekend right before the Fourth."

She looked skeptical. "You have a business

of your own and you've already done enough."

He didn't want to hear this again. "Cari, can I give you some advice?"

"I guess so."

"You need to learn how to accept help."

She looked confused and surprised. "I thought I was learning. But I also need to learn to do things myself, my way. It's part of what my financial advisor calls 'tough love.'"

Rick wondered when this woman had last received some old-fashioned tender loving care. "Can't we reach a compromise? You want to get your business going and the rest of us want this house to be in good working order—we have an agenda there. It benefits all of us to keep this street clean and fresh for our visitors, right?"

"Right." She crossed her arms and looked down at her sneakers. "I don't know. I guess I can't snap my fingers and make it all pretty. Maybe it would be better to bring in more help."

"Then let me gather some people together, to show you we can do it. And to show Doreen she doesn't own everyone in this town. If we stand up to her together, maybe she'll get the message and back off."

"You'd do that for me?"

The doubt in her eyes and her words undid him. "Of course I would."

She slanted her gaze toward him. "I'll never understand you, Rick."

"Nothing to understand. I just want to help you."

He couldn't tell her that he might want more than that. Much more. He wanted to help a friend; he was sincere in that. But he also wanted to show her that she could trust other people to not only help her, but to hold her up when she felt she was falling. He wanted her to know that God thought she was worth helping.

And he had another reason for reaching out to Cari Duncan. He was beginning to care about her. A lot.

He watched as a whole slew of emotions clouded her eyes. She'd been out there alone in the big world for so long, she'd forgotten what sticking together was all about. Maybe she'd forgotten that once she had been treasured and loved, too. She needed to feel that way again.

As if finally seeing his point, she said, "You know, I've missed this. I'd forgotten about the sense of community that comes with a church family. My father turned against me when I needed him the most. That's a hard lesson to get over. I don't know how to ask for help because I've trained myself not to expect help."

Rick took her hand in his as they stood there with workers buzzing all around. "Then maybe it's time you learned a new lesson. There's no shame in letting others support you along the way. That's how communities are built. That's what holds this town together."

"But not everyone is as kind as you and your family."

"True, but the good far outweighs the bad."

"I hope so. I sure hope so."

A sander cranked up and she motioned him back outside. "Okay, so what did you have in mind?"

Rick pumped his fist in the air. "I'm going to call in some reinforcements to get started on the upstairs. Let me talk to Rod about it, clear things with him and his crew so we don't mess up their work schedule or get in their way. But I think we can make this work and get things moving a whole lot faster for you."

She smiled up at him. "Okay."

For the first time, Rick saw real hope shining in her eyes. And that hope made her look even more beautiful.

Chapter Twelve

Over the next week, Cari felt as if she were on one of the home-improvement shows where they promised to rebuild a house in seven days. Her life was suddenly filled from dawn to dusk with burly workmen and well-meaning friends.

Once Rick had put out the word about helping Cari to renovate Duncan House, people had started showing up, some bringing their own tools, some offering to make sandwiches or run to the hardware store for more supplies, some just there to observe the commotion.

Rick had been careful to work around Mr. Green and the paid contractors, letting them do what they needed to do to bring everything up to code. And that included everything from the electricity to the plumbing.

But the thousand other little odd jobs—Rick and his teams were handling that. The quest to save Duncan House had become the buzzword around here. Jolena even had a sign in the window of the diner, asking for volunteers.

The formidable Mrs. Paula Meadows had deemed the house worthy of the historical society's attention, too. She had the garden club working on landscaping plans while she herself searched for authentic antiques to display in Cari's shop.

"Your mother was a dear lady. *She* had class," Paula had told Cari in a tight whisper. "We're doing this in her honor and we'd love to name the garden after her. When you have your grand opening, we'll do an official dedication ceremony." Then she'd leaned close, her expression bordering on distaste. "That should show certain people what a true Duncan is made of. You're your mother's daughter after all."

Cari had been so touched she could only nod and smile. Her mother would have loved this.

It was so amazing.

"Why are they doing this?" Cari finally asked Jolena one morning after the downstairs gleamed sparkling and new. Everything from the painted walls to the rebuilt kitchen cabinets shimmered and glistened with a fresh new face.

Jolena gave her a cockeyed look then grinned. "You *have* been away too long. This is how we operate here, honey. We stick together."

"Rick told me the same thing." She smiled then hugged her friend. "How could I have forgotten that?"

Jolena patted her back. "You're back now and you've found hope again. That's what matters."

If Cari thought back, she could remember her parents having just such friends. People who'd show up at the drop of a hat to lend a hand. She'd been so caught up in her resentment and her bitterness, she'd stayed away. And missed out on so much, including much of her father's last days.

Her reasons for staying away still haunted her, however. While Doreen had been quiet over the past week or so, Cari had heard rumors that she was fuming with anger at the way people had rallied around Cari. She fully expected the woman to gather a posse to make Cari cease and desist. She wouldn't be able to relax until she knew Doreen would leave her alone for good.

Today, the youth group from church was upstairs under Rick and Gayle's supervision, putting up new baseboards and drywall in the turret room. They'd made progress earlier today with Rick's guidance and Mr. Green constantly checking on their efforts to make sure the room was renovated to look like the original again. Now they were priming the walls so Cari could paint them later this week.

The old stairs had been reworked and mended all the way up to the second-floor landing. They were now solid and smelled of fresh wood. She planned to stain the banisters once the dust had settled and she had more elbow room. Maybe this weekend.

Heading up them now, she found Brady busy with some other kids upstairs. Rick was showing them how to put the primer on so it wouldn't be too heavy.

"Hi, Brady," she called, waving to him. He'd been here just about every day, quietly doing whatever needed to be done.

He looked embarrassed but waved back.

Cari walked over, admiring the big wall they'd finished in the flat white earlier today. "Good job, kids. I really appreciate this."

Brady looked away. Was he avoiding her?

"How you been?" she asked, playfully slapping him on the arm. "We haven't had much time to talk."

"Good." He turned back to his work on one of the turret room panels.

"Everything okay?"

He nodded but didn't look at her. Cari was about to walk away when he spoke. "I'm not supposed to be here."

Understanding dawned in her mind. "Because of your mother?"

"Yeah. She told me to stay away, but she had to go over to the next town to finish up a deal on a house she sold. She's fit to be tied about all of this."

Cari didn't doubt that. Knowing she was getting to Doreen should bring her a sense of pleasure, but it didn't. Not when she knew Brady could get in trouble for helping.

"And where's Bridget today?"

"In Atlanta, shopping with her friends. She said she hates driving up First Street—too congested these days."

Cari didn't comment on that, but she had to smile. So Bridget, in her infinite wisdom, went into the city just to avoid all of this. The logic was compelling.

Telling herself to take the high road, she turned to Brady. "So they don't know you're here."

"No. I kind of snuck out again. Mom probably hears that I've been helping, but so far she hasn't asked me about it."

Cari admired his fortitude, but she didn't want to get him in any more trouble with those two. "Thanks for coming, but maybe you'd better finish up and get home before they do."

He shrugged. "It's okay. I mean, I don't care what they say. I'm here with the youth group anyway. I like helping. And I like this house."

Some of the other boys snickered. One of them said, "Yeah, he likes it a lot."

"Shut up," Brady snapped, giving the kid a warning glance.

"Hey, cut that out." Rick thumped one of the boys on the head. "Keep at it. We've only got an hour of daylight left."

The boy who'd made the remark shot Rick a harsh glance then gave Brady a fuming look. "Yeah, whatever."

Rick's perturbed expression made the boy go back to work. "They've been at each other all afternoon."

"Why?" Cari asked. "This is a church group, right?"

"Right, but that doesn't mean everyone is sweetness and light. It's Youth Week and we're trying to bring them out of their self-absorbed little worlds to show them how to be responsible. We took them to the food bank yesterday to pack canned goods and deliver them to the area senior citizens. I thought I was going to have a food fight on my hands with that one." He indicated the boy who was still giving both Rick and Brady deep scowls. "Jeff—a hard case."

Cari watched the boy, noticing he kept eyeing Brady. Brady gave the boy several pointed looks in return. What was up with those two? "Maybe it's a girl," she said to Rick.

"Isn't it always?"

His smile made her almost drop her paint-brush. They'd been here like this, working side by side for the past few days, and she was beginning to like it way too much.

She also liked the way they managed to sit and eat together, usually something from Jolena's Diner. His tab had to be sky-high by now, since Rick insisted on feeding the workers most nights.

And he also insisted on staying late after everyone else left. Cari wasn't complaining. She enjoyed having him around.

"It's coming along, isn't it?" he asked now as he stood back to look at the bare canvas of the newly painted walls. "Do you plan to put paint in here, or some wallpaper, too?"

"Maybe wallpaper in the bathroom. But I think here in the bedroom, I want a two-toned effect. The darker blue under the chair railing and the powder blue on the rest. I have a beautiful blue-and-yellow floral quilted throw that'll look good with those colors. And I'll get pillows and bedding to match. Then a nice cushioned seat on the window seat in the turret room. I want it to look like spring in here, all light and airy. Hydrangeas, lots of hydrangeas in the patterns, to match my mother's old bush by the front porch."

She stopped, realizing he'd gone very still beside her. "What is it?"

Rick leaned close, his face inches from hers. "I love hearing you talk about this old place. Your eyes light up and you just get so beautiful."

Cari's blush burned a path down her neck. "I'm happy. Really happy. And I have you to thank for that."

"Me?" He grinned so widely she thought she might fall against the wet wall. "I make you happy?"

Yes, he did. "You've made a lot of this possible, organizing people to work in shifts, bringing everything together. Mr. Green has his crew downstairs and you're doing a lot up here. Teamwork—that's something I'm not that familiar with."

"Oh, so my *teamwork* abilities make you happy?"

"That's part of it, yes." How could she explain to him? And how could she give in to him? Her feelings for Rick scared her more than any confrontation she'd ever had with Doreen. "You've been a real friend, Rick. Amazing considering how we didn't really know each other that well before."

"I knew you," he said, his tone low. "You mentioned you had a crush on me in high school, right?

"Did I mention that? I don't remember."

"Yes, you do. And it's okay. I like knowing that." Before she could protest, he held up a finger. "But there's something I never told you. I never told anyone."

Her heart grew as heavy as her paintbrush. "What?"

"I kind of had a thing for you, too."

Cari shook her head. "No way. You were always with that snobby cheerleader."

"I might have been with her, but every time I'd see you I'd always wonder what was behind that shy smile. And now I know. And I like it."

Cari swallowed, trying to find air. Punching at her chest with a finger, she said, "This me you see right here, this is a whole new me."

"Maybe. We've both grown up a lot, I think. But I believe you were there—the real you—under all that shyness the whole time. And now, you've found your footing and let me tell you, nobody can compete with you. You're one of a kind, Princess."

"One of a kind? That can be good or bad, depending on how you look at things."

He looked down at her, his gaze moving over her face. "Well, from where I'm standing, it's all good. Trust me."

Cari gazed up at him and saw the truth in his eyes. He was being honest with her. "Thank you."

"Thank you? That's all I get?"

"What else do you expect me to say? Thank you for making me feel so happy.

Thank you for forcing me to accept help. Thank you for apple pie and sunshine and mountain air."

"You can thank Jolena for the pie and the good Lord for the sunshine and the mountain air. But I appreciate your vote of confidence on my persuasive techniques, I think."

"No, I mean it," she replied. "You're the real deal, Rick."

He glanced around then lowered his head. "I want to kiss you."

Shocked, Cari stole a glance at the kids and Rick's mom on the other side of the room. "That's not going to be easy in this crowd."

"I'll stay to help you clean up," he said, his tone so relaxed and reasonable she had to wonder if he ever lost his cool.

She was sweating bullets here. "Thanks again."

"And when we're alone, really alone, I'll still want to kiss you. But you don't have to thank me for that."

"Is that a warning?"

"No, ma'am, that's a declaration. I've wanted to kiss you for a very long time now." When she didn't say anything, he asked, "Do you want to kiss me?"

Oh, did she ever! She looked down. "Uh, well, yes."

"Good, then let's get the rest of this primer slapped on here and herd these kids out for pizza. We've got plans for later. Big plans."

Cari didn't think she could lift the brush back to the windowsill. Her hands were shaking too much. Rick Adams wanted to kiss her—Cari Duncan.

She was so caught up in that, she forgot time. All she saw was a great pristine white wall that mirrored a fresh new beginning in her own life. All she heard was Rick laughing and talking to his mother and the kids behind them. She managed to finish priming her spot, her eyes seeing white dots because she couldn't look at anyone for fear this was just a dream.

"Miss Cari?"

She pivoted to where a young girl stood smiling with pride in the arched door to the turret room. Cari stopped and stared, tears welling in her eyes. "It's beautiful. So beautiful."

Her little turret room was once again intact, complete with new windows that looked like the originals. Memories poured through her in the same way the last rays of sun were pouring through the glass. It was whitewashed with primer, clean and pretty, even if it was bare. The little room had been stripped clean, purged and rebuilt. Renewed.

Cari knew that feeling.

"It's perfect," she managed to say.

The girl pointed toward where Brady stood with paint all over him. "Brady said we needed to get this finished today."

Cari walked over to Brady. "Thanks, Brady. Now I can finish painting it and put some furniture in there. It's very pretty."

"It's very pretty, Brady," one of the other boys mimicked.

Jeff—the same boy who'd been picking on Brady before.

Gayle quickly herded them together. "Time to head to the Pizza Haus. C'mon. I have to have all of you back at the church by nine-thirty."

Brady glared at the other kid. "Stop it, Jeff."

Jeff made a face. "You started it."

"Hey," Rick said, getting between them. "Whatever's going on, drop it, right now. We're here to help Cari, not hurl insults at each other."

Jeff waved a hand toward Brady. "But he—"

"Now," Gayle said, pulling Jeff by his old

T-shirt. "Downstairs and outside. Leave your brushes in the bucket of water by the back door and leave any other supplies on the back porch."

The boys and girls gathered their things and trooped downstairs, Jeff and Brady still giving each other heavy scowls.

"What in the world is going on with those two?" Cari said to Rick after their footsteps echoed down the steps.

"Hormones?" He shrugged. "Maybe Jeff is teasing Brady because he knows you're kind of his big sister."

"Could be. But they seem so hostile."

"Again, like you said, might be a woman involved."

"But not a girlfriend-type woman," Cari replied. "I wonder if Bridget has been fussing at Brady about me. He told me that she and Doreen don't know he's here tonight."

"He had to sneak here to help you? That is bad."

"That's how those two operate. They aren't kind to anyone who threatens them."

"Are you a threat to them?"

She thought about that. "I'm not purposely trying to be. I just want to get the place ready to open my shop and live my life. As long as they stay clear of me, I'll do the same with them." That old need to get even had died down in the face of so many kind people willing to help her. "I don't think they're worth my time."

"I agree. You can be civil, but you don't have to be around them unless it's necessary."

"I can live with that." She poked at his ribs. "Especially when I'd rather spend time with you."

Rick let out a gasp. "She admitted she likes me. She really likes me."

Cari burst out laughing. "Yes, I like you. There. Are you happy now?"

He pulled her close. "I will be. Now about that kiss?"

She shook her head. "If I'm getting kissed tonight, I want to take a bath and get all gussied up."

"But you look so cute in those baggy cutoff jeans and that Georgia T-shirt."

She pushed at his chest. "A woman has her pride, you know. I don't think you've actually seen me in a dress."

He finished putting lids back on the paint cans. "Oh yes, I have. That pretty green one you wore to church. My favorite. Will you wear it—for our kiss?"

She was sure she was blushing. "I'll be glad to."

"Okay, then it's a date. I'll go get cleaned up and meet you back here. Remember that great little Italian place just outside of town? We could go there for a late dinner?"

"*Is* this a date?"

"I guess it is. If I have to get all cleaned up, might as well make the most of it."

"Good."

"But," he said, and tugged her back into his arms, "how about a peck to hold me until later?"

He didn't give her time to stop him. Instead, he feathered her face with light-weight kisses.

She giggled, her heart hammering a joyful beat. "Go. Now. I want Italian food."

"And I want that kiss."

"I don't think that'll be a problem."

Cari hurried downstairs to thank the last of the workers then waved goodbye to Rick as he passed by, his smile full of promise.

Humming, she hurried to get her things so she could take a shower and put on her green dress. She just might have to pull out a nice pair of shoes, too. She'd saved a few of her favorite ones for special occasions.

Thank You, God, she said as she danced around. *Finally, my life might be coming together.*

This was better than any fairy tale. Way better.

She just hoped reality didn't ruin the whole thing.

Chapter Thirteen

An hour later, Cari heard a knock at the door.

Thinking it was Rick, she hurried from the bathroom to the front of the house and tugged open the door.

But no one was there.

"Rick?"

She thought she heard a noise in the hydrangea bush so she leaned out over the porch railing. And felt something wet and mushy hitting her in the stomach.

Gasping, Cari stepped back and watched as an overripe tomato slid down the front of her dress. "What—?"

The echo of footsteps running away sounded from the street. Sprinting down the steps, Cari saw a shadowy figure heading around the corner. "Wait a minute!"

Did she dare chase after them?

Headlights on the street blinded her. Rick pulled the Jeep up to the curb and hopped out. "Hey, you must be as anxious as I am…."

He stopped when he saw her dress, his hands grabbing at her arms. "Cari, are you all right?"

She shook her head. "Not really. I have to go change."

Rick guided her up the steps. "What happened?"

She wiped at her soiled dress. "Someone threw a rotten tomato at me."

"You're kidding."

She pointed to the remains of the tomato splattered on the planked floor. "No, I'm very serious. I heard a knock at the door and thought it was you. But when I came out, someone was hiding in the bushes. They threw the tomato then I saw them running away."

He glanced out at the street. "Did you get a good look?"

"No. They were wearing a black hoodie— and whoever it was took off pretty fast." She didn't dare tell him that she'd caught just a glimpse of blond hair falling out from the hoodie the person was wearing.

Rick took her by the hand and ushered her into the house. "I don't get this. Who would do something so stupid and mean?"

But Cari got it. "Like I told you before, I think I know who's doing it. First the spilled paint and the message on the wall. And now, a tomato in my face. Can't you see it has to be Doreen or Bridget?"

Rick looked skeptical. His eyebrows shot up in disbelief. "Cari, this is so juvenile it's laughable. I can't believe two grown women would be so callous."

Heading into the kitchen, she said, "Well, I can." She grabbed a dish towel and wet it then tried to scrub the slimy tomato juice off her dress. "I lived with them for close to two years, Rick. This kind of thing happened to me a lot back then."

Rick shook his head. "You mean they played pranks on you?"

"All the time." Throwing the towel down, she dropped her hands to her sides. She hated the humiliating memories, but he needed to understand. "The worst fight my father and I had was because of those two. Over a pair of shoes, of all things. Bridget wanted to wear my sandals on the same night I wanted to wear them. When I protested, things turned very ugly. My father sided with Doreen and Bridget and I looked like a selfish, spoiled brat for not wanting to share with my sister. She got my shoes and I lost my father."

"I can't believe your dad would turn against you like that—because of a fight over shoes."

"It wasn't about the shoes," she said, the old frustrations coloring her words. "It was about how I was treated—like a stranger in my own home. It was like living in a prison. Bridget paraded her friends around, giggling and poking fun at me. She stole my things then denied everything. And I always came off looking jealous and petty." She hugged her hands to her midsection, the wet stickiness of the tomato making her sick. "And I'll look that way now if they have their say."

He stared at her as if he couldn't comprehend what she was telling him. "I've never heard of that. Whenever a widower remarries, I always think that's a good thing. I wish my mother could find someone, but she seems to like being on her own. I'm sorry your father's second marriage brought you so much heartache. And frankly, I can't understand why anyone would be so shallow and cruel."

Cari dropped her hands to her sides then lowered her head. "It threw me, too. And I didn't handle it very well. So finally, I just gave up and went off to college, hoping things would get better. But they never did. I'd come home on breaks and get the same treatment and it just got worse.

"After one of our famous fights, my father told me not to come back home until I could grow up and behave with a more civil attitude. So I didn't come back until he was too sick to care. After he died, I planned to never return, but here I am."

"And you think they've taken up where they left off?"

"Yes, I do. Doreen warned me to stay away from her children and if she found out Brady was here tonight, well, I guess this is her way of dealing with me." She started up the stairs. "And as for Bridget, she has a major crush on you. I'm a threat to her."

He looked up at her, shocked. "I don't care about Bridget."

"Maybe you should try telling her that."

Running a hand through his hair, he let out a sigh. "It can't be that bad. Maybe you're imagining things because you're still so angry at them."

Cari was in no mood to defend herself, especially to him. She'd hoped he'd understand, that he truly would be her champion in this. But in spite of all he'd done for her, he didn't get it. Hadn't she learned that she had to stand on her own? She intended to stand up to Doreen this time, no backing down or running away.

And that might cause problems with Rick. His sense of right and wrong didn't provide for such conniving people as Doreen and her daughter.

"I didn't imagine that ugly message suggesting I need to leave. And I didn't imagine this ruined dress. I'm going to change." With that, she hurried upstairs to the small bedroom where her things had been moved during the renovations.

It hurt that Rick doubted her, but then he had no way of knowing the wrath of these people. No one did. They hid it all well, unless Cari was around.

"How can I prove I'm right, Lord?" she asked, hoping for divine guidance. She wasn't sneaky enough to set up a scene where she actually had witnesses. And knowing Doreen and Bridget, they'd be very sure that didn't happen anyway. Rick was right; it was hard to imagine two grown women acting out in such a ridiculous way. But Cari suspected they'd go to any lengths to send her packing. Doreen wanted the property this house sat on and Bridget wanted the man who'd been kind to Cari. End of discussion.

By the time she'd changed into jeans and a clean white button-up shirt, Cari wasn't really in the mood for a romantic dinner. But Rick was waiting for her at the bottom of the stairs.

"I'm sorry," he said, taking her hand. "I loved that dress. Is it salvageable?"

"I'll take it to the cleaners tomorrow," she said, trying to find the happiness they'd shared earlier. "I hope so. It was one of the few I kept when I sold most of my clothes." She didn't tell him that once she would have probably worn the dress a couple of times before sticking it in the back of her closet. Now she treasured it. Just another lesson she'd learned the hard way—to guard her real treasures and appreciate what she had.

"You look great anyway." He held her hand in his then looked up into her eyes. "Can we start over?"

Pushing at her bad mood, Cari nodded. She

could tell he was still too shocked to believe her accusations. "I'm not overreacting, Rick. I know they're behind this. They think if they upset me enough, I'll run away like I did before. But this time, I'm not backing down. And if that means a confrontation, then I say bring it on."

His expression turned serious. "What if things get even worse for you? Cari, you could be in real danger living here on First Street. The town is fairly safe, but you're exposed here. There's a lot of late-night foot traffic through here, especially in the tourist seasons of summer and Christmas."

"I'll be fine," she said, touched that he was worried even if he did seem doubtful. "I'm having an alarm system installed for that very reason."

"But that's not until next week," he reminded her. "What if something else happens?"

"I'll deal with it," she said. "I'm okay. Mad about my dress, yes, and mad that someone would be so stupid in the first place, but I'll be all right."

"My brother keeps my dog out at the ranch. I could bring him to stay with you for a while. Of course, he's just a big old sappy golden retriever."

"I'll be okay. Let's go eat. I'm starving."

"Maybe you should at least report this to the cops."

"And have them laugh at me for getting hit with a tomato? No thanks. They'll just chalk it up to pranksters. They'd never investigate Doreen. She carries a lot of clout in this town."

"Well, so do I," he replied. "I'll go with you."

"No. It's all right." Pushing him toward the door, she said, "Hopefully, this won't happen again. As much as I want to confront them, if I just ignore them maybe they'll take the hint and give up."

But if Doreen was behind these pranks, she'd never give up. Cari didn't think even Doreen would dare try anything completely criminal, but she shivered all the same as she locked the front door.

She noticed Rick had cleaned the tomato off the porch. The man knew the way to a woman's heart. He took care of every detail before she'd even thought about it. But with Rick, it wasn't all about control the way it could be with some men. No, with him, it was just the polite, gentlemanly way to do things. His mama had raised him right, as

Jolena would say. And that was why he had a hard time seeing the bad in anyone. His one big flaw, Cari decided.

He opened the Jeep's door and helped her in. "You don't mind the top down, do you?"

"No, not at all." She needed some fresh air. The warm night wind cooled her burning skin.

As the Jeep whirled up the street toward the restaurant, Cari noticed a group standing near a fountain in the main square. "Hey, that was Brady and his friends. I thought they had to go back to the church."

Rick glanced in the rearview mirror. "They might be finished eating pizza. Maybe the chaperones gave them permission to hang out in the square."

"Maybe." Cari wondered again why Brady and Jeff had been so hostile toward each other earlier, since they seemed to be huddled together talking with the others now.

And she wondered why Brady had glanced up to give them a fixed stare as they'd driven by.

Rick's idea of a romantic evening had gone down the tubes as fast as a rafter taking on a spot of rapids. Having a tomato thrown at you could ruin any good mood, he figured. No matter how hard he tried to get back to the good feelings they'd shared earlier, Cari remained quiet and brooding. He hated seeing her this way, especially over two women who, according to her, were as shallow and self-centered as they came.

"Hey, you didn't eat much of your lasagna. I'll get a to-go box."

"No, don't," she said, pushing her plate away. "I'm not very hungry."

Dropping his fork, Rick reached for her hand. "Don't do this. Don't let them win. If Doreen was behind what happened and you're letting it get to you this way, then she wins. You know that saying about what angers you controls you? Don't let her control you, Cari."

She glanced up at him, her eyes glistening with pent-up frustration. "She's been in control since the day she pranced into my father's real estate office, pretending to be looking for a job. That's just the way it is."

"Not if you can rise above her shenanigans."

"And how am I supposed to do that? I've asked God to show me the way. I've prayed for strength and patience. I came back here with a hope of finding my home again, but already I'm beginning to regret that decision. I think I came home too late. Way too late."

Rick didn't know how to reach her. "Have you asked God to show you how to forgive? Maybe you've been praying for the wrong things. Maybe you came home for the wrong reasons."

She put a hand to her mouth. "How do I forgive someone who doesn't know the meaning of the word? This woman goes to church each Sunday, but she's evil, Rick. She always twisted the truth to make my father side with her and that tactic caused him to turn on me. How can I justify forgiving that?"

Rick tried again. "Her fate isn't in your hands. If all you say is true, she'll be judged in due time. But don't let her steal your happiness or your chance to be the better person. You have a lot of people supporting you. We're all behind you, Cari. Maybe you should try focusing on that instead of pouring all your energy into this one negative aspect of your life."

She put her head down, her hand on her chin. For a long time, she just sat there looking over at him, her eyes full of a deep hurting pain. Then she finally lifted up, her hands on the table. "You're right. I'm been blessed by all the incredible kindness I've received since I came back. And I don't take that lightly, honestly I don't. But you have to understand, when Doreen married my father, my self-esteem was already low. I'd just lost my mother and my daddy had become distant and depressed. He only married Doreen because he was so distraught about my mother, he didn't grasp what was happening to him. She used his vulnerabilities to take over his life. And once she was inside our home, she took over my life, too. She pitted Bridget against me at every turn. Brady was the only saving grace. He was too young to understand what was going on. And he looked up to me because his sister treated him so badly. We bonded right away, but I can't keep that bond. Doreen will see to that. She'll make sure Brady turns against me, too. She'll keep at it until—"

Rick saw the fear there in her eyes and instantly understood what she was trying to tell him. "You're afraid she'll turn everyone—even me—against you, aren't you?"

Her nod was so brief he almost missed it.

But Cari had confirmed her worst fears with that tiny gesture. And like any human being, she didn't want to be alone and isolated again.

Rick's heart opened as he accepted his feelings for her. She'd been a princess once but she'd become an ousted princess, trapped in a tower of loneliness and isolation, banished to a foreign land, away from everyone and everything she loved.

Could he rescue her?

"Cari," he said, pulling her up and into his arms. "I'll never abandon you. God hasn't abandoned you. We're both right here. Do you hear me?" When she didn't answer, he lifted her chin so he could see her face. "Cari, do you believe me?"

She swallowed, her eyes misty and fathomless. "I want to believe you, so much. But you don't owe me anything, Rick. You're just being a good neighbor, a good friend. Because you've become a good man. I only hope I can live up to all that potential you seem to think I have."

He tugged her out of the restaurant, pulling her toward the Jeep. When they reached the vehicle, he turned her around and brought her back into his arms. "I care about you, okay? No matter what, remember that."

The only way he knew to make her see was to show her. So he lifted her chin with his hand and he pulled her toward him, his lips touching hers in a soft, sweet need. That sweet need swept through him like a rushing river, bonding him to her in a purging acceptance.

Cari fell against him, returning the same need, her lips sighing against his. She lifted away but held him close. "I don't deserve you. I'd hate to lose our friendship. You've been so kind to me."

"It's not just about being kind," he said. "It's about so much more between us." Then he pulled back to stare down at her. "I want to kiss you again, but not like this. I want things between us to be special and I want you to be sure. Just hold on to what we felt tonight. And then, whenever you're ready, you let me know how you feel, okay?"

She bobbed her head then hopped up into the Jeep. They drove the short distance to her house in silence. Rick walked her to the door. "Let me come in and check around."

He didn't wait for her permission. He walked through the old, creaking house, turning on lights and checking locked doors and windows. "Looks okay down here. Let's check upstairs."

She followed him without a word as he turned on lights in each of the rooms upstairs. When they reached the turret room, he flipped on the hanging chandelier, watching as light cascaded across the brilliant white-washed walls.

And heard Cari's gasp behind him.

He looked back and saw her finger going up in the air toward the turret.

Rick turned and looked at the little octagonal room.

And saw what Cari had seen.

Two of the brand-new windows had been shattered into pieces. Glass covered the window seat and the floor.

And two big rocks lay amid the crushed, broken glass.

Without a word, Cari rushed back down the stairs.

But the echo of her angry steps ricocheted throughout the empty rooms with an eerie cadence that confirmed what she'd believed all along. Someone was definitely trying to send her a message. Rick hoped he could find out who before Cari took matters into her own hands.

Chapter Fourteen

"Yes, I need two new windows installed. Yes, the turret room," Cari explained one more time to Rod Green. "I know, I know. We just finished those two days ago." When she told him what had happened, she had to hold the phone away from her ear. The man didn't like having to repeat the same tasks, especially when it involved vandalism and destruction of property. "I agree, Mr. Green. It's sad and it's not fair, but I need those windows replaced. As soon as possible."

She hung up the phone, drained and discouraged, wondering for the hundredth time if she should leave Knotwood Mountain and never come back.

But what about your father?

The voice inside her head echoed through

her tired system. Would she be dishonoring her father if she sold the property and left? What did that matter now, she wondered. She'd dishonored him while he was alive, because she was too hurt and too prideful to come home and fight for him.

Thinking she could have helped him, Cari wished she could change things and turn back the clock to make it right.

Then stay here and fight now.

Did she have the stamina, the strength to do that?

What if Rick got tired of her bitterness and turned on her the way her father had? Cari knew that would break her heart. And right now, her heart was too fragile to take much more.

Remembering how she'd asked him to leave the other night after finding the broken windows, Cari figured Rick had already had enough. She hadn't talked to him in the past couple of days, but the lasting memory of their kiss had stayed with her, reminding her that he cared about her.

Still, she couldn't think about that right now. Now that most of the downstairs had been painted and polished and the alarm system was ready to go, she could finally move the rest of her inventory out of storage and into the shop. Maybe she could lose herself in working on her jewelry designs. That had always brought her joy and working helped to keep her calm and centered. She'd focus on that and put the need to confront Doreen out of her mind.

Grabbing her cup of coffee, Cari walked out onto the big porch, her spirits lifted by the new landscaping. Mrs. Meadows and her formidable team had done a great job of cleaning up the shrubs and weeds. Now the front path leading to the newly painted steps was lined with daylilies and hosta plants. The old crape myrtle by the steps had been pruned and trimmed so that the branches cascaded out like an umbrella offering shade. And the hydrangeas had been shaped and nurtured, their cotton-candy blue and pink blossoms and wide green leaves shining brightly in the morning sun.

She stepped off the porch to admire the new sign that had been delivered yesterday. Hometown Princess. She liked that name for her boutique. It summed her up. And Rick called her a princess all the time, whether she truly was one or not. The wide white sign held deep purple scrolled letters, its border etched with grapevines and flowers. It was dainty and pristine but with a bit of attitude. And she sure needed attitude to pull this off.

Maybe I can learn from the sign, she thought, smiling to herself in spite of her worries.

"It looks good."

Cari whirled to find Brady standing behind her. "Thanks." She motioned him forward. "What are you up to today?"

He shrugged. "Just hanging out. I'm on restriction because—" He stopped, dropped his head.

"Because you came here the other night and helped me with the house?"

Cari knew the answer from his guarded expression. "Mom was pretty hot when she found out. You know how people like to talk around here."

"Yes, I do." Cari sat down on the steps. "I'm sorry you got in trouble. Maybe you shouldn't be seen talking to me."

"I don't care," he said, his tone full of determined pride. "Bridget gets away with everything and…I'm always in trouble."

"I can certainly understand that." Cari didn't dare tell him that his family had made her life miserable. "Sometimes it's hard to

just live your life when you've got other
people telling you what to do."

He lifted his head. "Yeah, that's it exactly.
They're always telling me how to behave,
what to wear. Mom worries about what
people will think." He shrugged. "She never
worries about what I think."

Cari's heart went out to the boy. He was at
that delicate cusp between youth and adult-
hood. That awkward, miserable age. The same
age she'd been when Doreen had come into
her life. "Wanna come in and have a Danish?
Got them fresh from Jolena this morning."

He glanced around. "Sure. Mom won't
let me drive since I'm on restriction. I have
to walk everywhere even though I have my
permit. Might as well hang out with you."

Cari lifted up to put a hand around his
shoulder, a disturbing thought crossing her
mind. What if some of Brady's friends were
harassing her? "You can always hang out with
me, okay? Remember that. And I have an
ulterior motive. You can help me unpack some
of my things for the shop. The shelves are up
and ready to display my treasures." Maybe
he'd clue her in on the kids he hung out with.

"Cool." He followed her up the steps and
into the house, his smile soft with gratitude.

After feeding Brady and giving him a glass of milk, Cari showed him the boxes lining the walls of the small storage room in the back of the house. "Now, be careful with these things," she cautioned. "The jewelry is delicate and we need to hang the necklaces on those old frames I have sitting on the counter. I'll show you how to hook them across the wires."

Brady nodded. "I hope none of my friends come by. They'd rag me for playing with necklaces and bracelets."

Cari tried to sound unconcerned. "Hey, you're helping me out. I'll even pay you for your time. And I might be able to hire a couple of your buddies, too."

He looked surprised, then cautious. "Really? I could use a summer job, but most of my friends are busy."

"Not a good idea to hire everyone, huh?"

He shook his head. "Probably not. And… I'd have to clear it with Mom."

She hadn't considered that. But she did need a stock boy and Brady would be perfect. "I hope she'll agree." Maybe if she begged Doreen. "I can only pay you minimum wage for now and only for a few hours each week. But if it works out and you're interested in working some after school, I might be able to increase that a little bit in the fall."

"That'd be great." He lifted a box and carried it to the front of the building. "So, Mr. Green's all done down here?"

"Yes, thank goodness." She brought another box up front. "They finished the final touches late last night." Then she made a face. "But…someone broke out two of the turret room windows. He's coming back later today to replace those."

Brady stopped, his hand on a box. "Really? When did that happen?"

Cari pulled out a dainty evening bag that she'd found in a flea market booth. She'd reworked it with rows of costume jewels—sapphires, rubies and emeralds—all marching across the white silk with glittering precision. "The other night, after the youth group was here. And after you all worked so hard on that room. I was so upset I almost gave up." She couldn't voice her suspicions. As much as she resented his mother, she wouldn't talk badly about the woman to her son. "But whoever's messing with me doesn't realize I'm not leaving Knotwood Mountain."

He busied himself with opening another box. "Do you…like…know who did it?"

"No, I don't." At least she couldn't be sure. "Rick said I should report it to the police, but I tried that the first time the place was vandalized and they didn't seem too concerned." She glanced out at the street. Already the tourist traffic had increased. Another week until the big Fourth of July weekend. She hoped she'd be ready for business by then. Turning back to Brady, she said, "I have an alarm system now. I can turn that on whenever I leave. And especially at night. That should stop the vandalism."

He didn't say anything, so she let him go back to unpacking the various items she'd either designed or ordered at market. Soon Cari was immersed in getting her stock in order, the joy of being able to do what she loved overtaking her worries about vandals. Brady worked with her, side by side, his quiet concentration on getting it right making her glad she'd offered him a job.

Two hours later, they'd cleared out most of the boxes from the storage room, but Brady hadn't divulged anything about his friends. Or himself, for that matter. Why did she get the feeling that maybe he did know something about the vandalism? Was he protecting his friends, or his sister?

"This place is beginning to look the way I envisioned it," she said as she offered him a soft drink. "With you helping, I got these things out in half the time it would have taken if I'd done it by myself. I sure do appreciate it."

Brady glanced around, clearly uncomfortable with the frilly blouses and flounce skirts. "Do women really like this stuff?"

"Some women do," she replied, her fingers trailing over a stuffed rack of clothes. "It's all about being unique and different. I try to keep my prices down, though. That way, I can deal in volume and, hopefully, turn a profit."

He took a long swig of his drink. "Yeah, Mom's always talking about making more money. Sometimes, she sits at her desk working on her computer until late at night."

"Your mother always did have a strong work ethic," Cari said. To the point of ignoring her own family, apparently. Then because she needed to know, she asked, "Does she do okay with her real estate—I mean now that the economy is so bad?"

"I guess," he said, shrugging. "She never talks to me about that stuff. Bridget spends money all the time, though. Mom fusses at her, but Bridget doesn't care."

Of that, Cari had no doubts. But she wondered about other things. "Brady, after I left, was my dad happy? I mean really happy?"

Brady's expression turned cautious and blank. He flipped his bangs and stared out the window, his empty drink can in one hand. "I guess. He…him and me didn't get along so well."

That surprised Cari. "But…he seemed to love all of you so much."

Brady kept staring out the window. "He was sick a lot. Sometimes, he got really nasty with us. He'd scream at Bridget a lot. And he argued with Mom about everything."

Hearing that her father fussed at Doreen should have brought Cari a measure of triumph, but it only left her feeling empty and hollow. Did she really wish her father the same misery she'd suffered? No, she couldn't wish that on anyone. But it hurt her to think he'd become as bitter as she'd been.

"Did he ever mention me?"

Brady turned at her question, his gaze sweeping over her. "Sometimes, after he got really bad off. He'd sleep on the couch in the den and he'd mumble things."

Tears pricked at Cari's eyes. "It's all right.

You don't have to talk about it. It's done now. I'm just glad I got to see him before he died."

"He asked for you all the time," Brady said. "That's why Mom finally called you. She didn't want to, but he kept asking."

Cari couldn't stop the tears. "He did?" She wiped at her eyes. "I never knew."

"I didn't mean to make you cry," Brady said, embarrassment coloring his freckled face. "I guess I need to go before Mom sends Bridget out looking for me."

Cari sniffed and wiped her face. "Don't mind me. I get emotional, thinking about my parents."

He went to the kitchen and threw his can in the recycling bin. "I guess it's hard, not having anyone."

Cari could only nod.

"I don't remember my dad. Mom wouldn't talk about him much. She said he was a loser and he wasn't worth discussing."

Ashamed of her own self-centered resentment, Cari had never once given thought to what Brady and Bridget must have gone through with their parents divorcing when they were so young. No wonder they both seemed to have issues. How could she blame them?

Walking with Brady toward the door, she put a hand on his shoulder. "I hope my daddy at least treated you better than that. He was a good father once. I'd like to believe he cared about all of us."

Brady bobbed his head. "I don't know. It's hard to say how he felt." Then he glanced around. "I need to go."

Cari opened the door. "If you want to come by for a couple of hours tomorrow, I could use the help. I'll write you a check at the end of the week."

"Sure."

They walked to the steps. "Thanks again," Cari said.

The sound of a car speeding up the busy street caused her to look up.

Bridget pulled up the short driveway and slammed on the brakes, the convertible skidding to an abrupt stop. "Brady, get in the car, right now. Mom is looking for you. And when I tell her where I found you—" She stopped, her harsh expression moving from Brady to Cari. "You think you can steal my little brother from me, too? Do you, Cari?"

Cari hurried down the steps to face her. "Brady helped me do some unpacking. I'm going to pay him for his time."

"Well, that's funny, considering you had to beg for a bank loan." Smirking at Brady, she said, "Better hurry up and cash that check. Because we all know you don't have a dime to your name. Now get in, Brady. I have a date tonight." She lifted her sunglasses. "With Rick Adams."

Cari's stomach went hot with pain. How could she believe a word coming out of Bridget's mouth? She wouldn't. She couldn't. "Thanks again for helping, Brady."

Brady shot Cari an apologetic look then hopped in the car. Bridget didn't give Cari time to say anything else. She peeled out and took off up the street, her blond locks fanning out behind her head.

But Cari saw the triumphant look Bridget shot her through the rearview mirror.

And she decided she'd had enough. Heading back inside, she grabbed her purse then made sure she set the new alarm.

It was high time she had a one-on-one talk with Doreen. It was time to get everything out in the open, so she could at least start the process of healing. She wanted to stay here and she wanted to get to know Rick better, regardless of how Bridget felt about that. And she wanted to be a good sister to Brady.

Because it was obvious that the kid needed someone in his life who actually cared about him enough to fight for him.

She'd just reached her car when Rick's Jeep pulled up to the curb. And he looked all dressed up and ready for a date.

Chapter Fifteen

Cari wouldn't ask. She refused to stoop to Bridget's level. Never mind that she and Rick had grown closer with each passing day. Never mind that he'd kissed *her.*

Had he kissed Bridget in that same way? The thought twisted her stomach in knots.

"Hi," he said, walking toward her, his smile as sure and steady as always. "I was passing through and saw you coming out of your door. How are you?"

"Fine," she said. "I was just leaving."

"And with such an intense frown on your face, too. Are you going to the banquet?"

Confused, she shook her head. "What banquet?"

He waited for a group of chattering twenty-somethings to pass by out on the sidewalk. "A dinner out at a catfish restaurant on the river south of town. One of the business associations sent me an invitation a couple of weeks ago. I'd almost forgotten about it until—"

"Until Bridget reminded you?" she asked, wishing she could put a muzzle on herself.

"Bridget?" Now he looked confused. "No, my mother reminded me. I would have called you to come with me, but I had to hurry and get cleaned up. I'd really rather not go, but duty calls."

Relief washed through Cari like a warm rain. "I didn't get an invitation, but then I'm not officially open for business yet." And she might not be welcome yet, either. She'd find that out when she finished things up and had her grand opening.

"Won't be long before you'll be just as involved in these things as I am," he said. He looked at his watch. "If you want to come with me…"

She should, just to show Bridget. But the high road beckoned to her. "No, no. I have an errand to run. You go ahead, since you're already dressed and ready." She wondered if Bridget had a seat waiting for him at the banquet. And she wondered if he was being ambushed. Did she dare tell him about

Bridget's declaration—that they had a date? No. That would make Cari look like a jealous shrew. Which wouldn't be too far from the truth, come to think of it.

He lingered for a minute then reached up to push a strand of hair off her face. "Hey, are you all right?"

"I'm great. Brady helped me unpack some of my stock this afternoon. Mr. Green has finished most of the tough renovation jobs. The plumbing down here is in better working order now and I have a new refrigerator and stove in the kitchen. I'm going to paint the cabinets later, I think. But as for the front of the place—these two rooms and the hallway—the boutique's coming together. And the alarm system is intact."

"No more trouble since the last time?"

She didn't want to tell him what Bridget had said to her. Or that she was about to go and confront Doreen. "No. All's quiet for now. Maybe it's over."

"I hope so. Only a few days until the Fourth."

"Yep. This summer is going by so fast."

He leaned close. "Well, I guess I'd better get to the restaurant before the fried catfish gets cold." He gave her a quick peck on the cheek. "Do you want to come out to the ranch tomorrow? I'll give you the grand tour and maybe we can go horseback riding?"

Cari thought about turning him down, but her heart told her to go on faith and trust that he didn't actually have a real date with Bridget. And since he'd just kissed her on the cheek, she was pretty sure she had the upper hand for now.

Stop thinking in that way, she told herself. She refused to get into a superficial competition with Bridget. Cari had made a lot of mistakes in her life, but she wasn't as petty and shallow as Bridget Stillman. And she prayed God would guide her to take that high road she was trying so hard to follow. "I'd like that," she said. "But maybe later in the day. I still have a lot to do around here in the morning."

He nodded, his hand touching hers. "I can help you."

"Rick, you have a store to run, remember?"

"Yeah, I guess I do at that. And tomorrow being a Saturday, we'll be pretty busy. But I have extra staff in place so I can take off early. That way, I can work most of the holiday weekend and give my employees time with their families."

Cari had never known a man like Rick Adams. He was dedicated, devout and thoughtful. He cared about other people and always put others first. Not only could she learn a lesson in business from him, she could also learn a lesson on humanity from him. "Then I guess I'll see you tomorrow afternoon," she said. "Now get going. I don't want you to miss out on your dinner."

"One more kiss," he said, tugging her close. This time, he touched his lips to hers long enough for Cari to sigh and hold him tight.

When he pulled back, she giggled. "We'll be the talk of the town."

"I think we already are," he said through a satisfied grin. "Doesn't bother me one bit."

She believed that. Nothing seemed to bother him.

Another lesson for her.

"Bye," she said, pushing him toward the Jeep. "Don't eat too much."

"They're having cheesecake for dessert," he shouted, hopping into the Jeep. Then he waved, winking at her, before he took off in the late-day traffic.

Cari watched him leave then sank down on the porch steps, all of her self-righteous steam suddenly gone.

What should I do, Lord? She sat there, silent and still, wondering if she should confront Doreen. Or maybe just talk to the woman about allowing Brady to work for her. What could be the harm in that?

Deciding she couldn't let her temper get the best of her, Cari got up and went back inside to unpack some more. She'd focus on her work here and hope there would be no more vandalism, especially since Mr. Green had done a rush job on fixing the windows in the turret room. And maybe Doreen would slowly come to accept that Cari was here to stay and give Cari a chance to be a friend to Brady.

So she cranked up the music on the local mixed music radio station, poured herself a tall glass of lemonade and became immersed in organizing the boutique, her thoughts centered on having her own date with Rick tomorrow afternoon.

Rick gave Bridget a brittle smile and carefully extracted her arm from his. He'd been set up, plain and simple. Somehow, Bridget and Doreen had managed to get him seated right next to them tonight. And now, only manners kept him from moving to another table. He had to wonder now why Cari had asked him if Bridget reminded him of this dinner. Had Cari known Bridget would be here?

"How's the fish?" Bridget asked, her eyes wide with wonder.

"Good." Rick dropped the direction of his thoughts and looked over at her chicken. He'd ask Cari about her comment tomorrow. "How's your meal?" he asked Bridget, trying to make small talk.

She shrugged, her dangling gold earrings looping around her shoulders. "You know— same old food, same old scene." She leaned close, her perfume stifling him. "We could skip out early. I only came because Mom insisted. And because she told me you'd be seated at our table."

Rick chuckled, sweat beading on his brow. "And I only came because my mother reminded me I'd reserved a seat and paid for my dinner."

Bridget's pout was immediate and completely fake. "And here I thought you came to see me."

"I didn't know you'd be here," he replied, wishing he'd just stayed at Cari's. They could have ordered pizza and unpacked trinkets. "A pleasant surprise," he said, hoping the Good Lord didn't strike him down for fibbing.

Bridget didn't quit. "Well, now that you're here and you see me sitting here, are you glad you came?"

How to answer that? "It's hard to say. These functions are usually boring. But I'm not bored tonight." No, he was too keyed up to be bored.

"Then you are glad to see me," Bridget said, sitting up to lean toward him. "But even though I'm with you, I'm very bored with all these stuffy old people. Let's go for a ride along the river road with the top down."

"You mean in your car?"

"Your car or mine. I don't care. I just want to get out of here before they start handing out the awards." She did a mock yawn. "We can be alone, finally."

Rick looked across the table at Doreen. She'd had her gaze centered on her daughter and him for most of the night. That is, when she wasn't flirting with the newly divorced car salesman sitting next to her. He was beginning to see Cari's point about these two. They were both a piece of work, smooth operators and definitely always on the prowl.

"Rick?"

He looked back at Bridget. "That sounds nice, really. But it would be rude of me to leave early, Bridget. The people who win these awards have worked hard to help make Knotwood Mountain a better place. We owe them the courtesy of staying here to share in the celebration. I won one myself last year and it was nice to look out over the audience and see the friendly faces."

"Oh, bother," Bridget said, her words exaggerated and harsh. "You sound just like my mother, always thinking about this stupid little town."

"Don't you care about your home?" Rick asked, hoping to sway her. "You know, we have a strong sense of community here. You should come to church sometimes, meet more people your own age. We have a great college-age group. They do all kinds of fun things together."

"Are you kidding me? I'll be twenty-four soon. The kids around here are so lame." She tossed her hair off her shoulder. "I don't do church and I don't hang out with Jesus freaks. And I can't wait to get out of here. Even if I can't go back to school this fall, I'm leaving this place one way or another." Then, her petulance gone for a moment, she smoothed her napkin in her lap. "Unless of course a certain store owner could convince me to stay."

Rick couldn't believe he'd once again gotten caught up in Bridget's little games. So she'd stay if he got involved with her? Like that was gonna happen. He had to extricate himself from this uncomfortable situation, but he refused to leave since she'd only follow him. Looking across the room, he said, "There's the mayor. I need to discuss a few things with her before the awards ceremony starts. Will you excuse me?"

He didn't give Bridget time to answer. Instead he got up and moved through the crowd until he'd made his way to where the mayor stood talking to another woman. After greeting the women and getting into a conversation that lasted a few minutes, he glanced back at the table where he'd been sitting.

Bridget was gone.

Rick hoped she was gone for the night. He breathed a sigh of relief then waited until the last possible moment before heading back to his seat. He shouldn't be so cowardly about this, but he didn't want to hurt Bridget. And he really wanted to be with Cari tonight. That was at the heart of the matter. If he made Bridget angry, she could make things worse for Cari.

Help me, dear Lord.

When he sat down, Doreen looked across at him then got up to come around the table. "She left." She shot him a hostile look. "You need to quit stringing my daughter along, Rick. Make a commitment, one way or another. You can't have both of them."

"What are you talking about?" he asked, his voice low.

Doreen shook her head. "Men are so dense sometimes. You know what I mean. Before Cari came back, you flirted with Bridget all the time. The girl thinks you care about her. And I had hoped…well, never mind what I hoped. I won't have you toying with my daughter's affections, especially since you seem to be over the moon about Cari." She stood to straighten her black dress. "We'll see how that turns out. Cari can be a handful but then you'll just have to see that for yourself. And you will, mark my words. And don't expect Bridget to be waiting in the wings for you when you come to your senses."

Rick stared up at her, shocked and feeling

sheepish. Had he been stringing Bridget along? Had she misread his attempts at kindness? "I'm sorry, Doreen. I thought Bridget and I were just friends."

"Well, you thought wrong." She shot him one last frown before returning to the other side of the table with a charming smile for her newest conquest.

Rick listened to the awards being announced, clapping at all the right moments while his mind raced, replaying every encounter he'd had with Bridget over the last few months. For the life of him, he couldn't see past just being polite to the girl but maybe he'd also been blinded to the truth, too. Then he thought again about how Cari had asked him if Bridget was the one who'd reminded him of the banquet tonight. Which meant Bridget had probably paid Cari a visit to purposely let her know they'd be here together tonight.

Great, Rick thought. I've really messed things up now. He should have stayed with Cari, regardless of making appearances and honoring the price of a meal. And it was high time he stood up to Bridget's not-so-subtle overtures toward a romance. He didn't want anything more with Bridget.

This had to stop. He needed to be honest with Bridget once and for all. At least he could agree with Doreen on that point. He'd called himself doing a good deed, trying to tolerate her so he could encourage her to come to church. But that had backfired on him, big-time. It had been easy to flirt with Bridget before, thinking it was harmless and hoping she'd change and find God's grace in the process.

But now, he cared about Cari too much to keep this up.

No, he more than cared about her. He was falling in love with her. And waffling on that wasn't fair to either Bridget or Cari. How could it be that he was always strong and decisive in his business dealings and whenever he dealt with family issues, but when it came to women, he caved like a big old teddy bear?

And that, my friend, is what got you so off track in Atlanta. Was this a pattern that would keep him from ever settling down with one woman? Not if he could help it.

He wanted one woman. He wanted Cari. On that he was sure, at least.

High time Bridget understood the boundaries so she'd stop tormenting Cari. He hoped. He didn't want to make things worse for Cari. Deciding he'd need to handle this situation with a lot of prayer and diplomacy, Rick listened to the rest of the ceremony then left as soon as the dinner was over, his thoughts centered on how to fix the situation he'd gotten himself into without hurting any delicate feminine feelings.

Especially Cari's delicate feminine feelings.

It was after midnight when Cari finished the last of her unpacking then stood back to admire the shelves lined with bold colorful jewelry, sequined and sparkling purses, bright floral scarves, sheer blouses and basic T-shirts. The big round racks centered in the middle of the room held dresses and sweaters, skirts and casual tops and bottoms. And an armoire on the far wall held even more accessories and trinkets, most of them her original designs and her refurbished estate jewelry.

She'd placed pieces of eclectic art around the few open walls to add some whimsy and charm to the furnishings and she'd put the two floral chairs she'd upholstered by the bay windows with an old round wicker table between them. She'd keep fresh flowers on the table as much as possible, maybe by cutting a deal with the florist around the corner.

Soon, she'd have her workshop installed upstairs in the tiny bedroom that had once served as a nursery. If the Lord was willing, she might even one day use that room for its original purpose again—a baby.

That train of thought jarred her. "Wow. First things first. Right now, this business is your baby."

So she changed her thoughts back to the here and now, her daydreams filled with a maternal longing all the same. She could almost picture Rick holding a tiny child.

"Stop that!" Cari whirled to admire the new and improved Duncan House.

Mr. Green and his workers had done an amazing job of cleaning up and renovating the bottom floor of the house. The kitchen still needed a lot of work, but he'd promised Cari he'd finish that part up after-hours and later when the high tourist season had settled down a bit. For now, the plan had been on getting the front hallway and the two main rooms ready for the boutique's opening next week. Now that that task was done, Cari couldn't help but be proud.

"It looks great," she told herself as she tidied up and got ready for bed. Exhausted but elated, Cari headed upstairs with a smile on her face. *Thank You, Lord, for providing me with such a blessing in Mr. Green. And thank You for all the help You sent to me to speed things up.* And Rick was the first one on that list.

She thanked God for Rick and his mother and Jolena and her helpful daughters. For Brady and the youth from the church, for the many well-wishers and neighbors who'd offered help, most of them doing it out of respect for her parents. Thinking she really did have a lot to be thankful for, Cari glanced into the turret room. The moonlight invited her inside the big empty room and since she was naturally drawn toward the round little structure in the corner, she padded over to sit in her favorite spot on the window seat.

The night outside was whitewashed in magnolia-colored moonbeams. The wind lifted the crape myrtle, causing the pink and purple blossoms to fall like lace down to the street below. She could hear the faint sounds of country music coming from the karaoke stage at the Pizza Haus, followed by the laughter of patrons out on the patio overlooking the river. It was nice, sitting here in her home, knowing she'd accomplished a lot over the last month or so. All the hard work was paying off at last.

Cari leaned down, her chin resting on her hands as she stared out into the night, her thoughts on Rick and how much she'd come to care about him. Did he feel the same? His kisses indicated he did.

But he'd spent the evening with Bridget.

Cari sat up, pushing her jealousy aside as she reminded herself Bridget hadn't been honest about their so-called date.

"And I won't fall into her traps," Cari said into the still house. "Never again."

She was turning to head to the small bedroom down the hall when she heard a car zooming up the street below. Glancing down, she watched as the driver of the car threw something into the air. When she heard a thud hitting her front porch, Cari gasped, her hand coming to her throat.

The motion-detector kicked on, lighting up the front yard and her newly installed alarm went off, the sound like a siren shrilling out over the quiet night. As she hurried back downstairs to hit the alarm button, Cari heard the car taking off, tires grinding against asphalt.

And she watched out the bay window as the white convertible sped away into the night.

Chapter Sixteen

Rick could tell something was wrong the minute he knocked on Cari's door the next afternoon. Did she think he'd been with Bridget last night?

You were with Bridget last night, he reminded himself as he took in all the pretty baubles in Cari's shop. But not in the same way he wanted to be with Cari—not in a serious "with her because he really wanted to be there" way. Of course, try telling that to a woman.

"Hi. Are you ready to head to the ranch?"

She nodded then motioned him in, her expression blank and guarded. "I will be in about five minutes."

Trying to gauge her mood, he said, "The place looks fantastic. You're gonna do great business here. Mom doesn't have anything like this in her apparel shop upstairs. We needed something young and hip like this."

"Yes, I think so."

Okay, not exactly the response he was searching for. He tried again. "So how's your morning been?"

She shrugged. "I've had a few phone calls asking when I'll be open and I've had people peering in the windows. The chamber of commerce did a piece in their weekly newsletter for the Sunday paper, so that's brought in some early lookers, too."

"That's a good sign."

She whirled then. "Yes, a very good sign. And speaking of signs, remember the one I had made, the sign that showed the name of my shop? You know, the one I so proudly hung on the front porch a couple of days ago?"

Rick noted the gradual rise in her words with each question she threw out. "Yes, I liked that sign a lot. What about it?"

She waved toward the porch. "Did you happen to notice it's not there today?"

He had not noticed that and now he was thinking probably that was a bad thing, not noticing. "Really? What happened? Did you take it down? Or did it fall? The hooks were solid so they should have held."

"Oh, they would have if someone hadn't come by late last night to purposely throw a brick right into my pretty sign. Knocked it off its hinges and it fell and hit one of my dish gardens and broke the clay pot and destroyed some of my flowers. The sign has a big, ugly gash across the front and one of the chains is broken. I have to have it repaired. And the brick landed on the planked floor and knocked out a hole about four inches wide right by the front door. But you probably didn't notice that either."

He'd have to learn to be more observant. "No, I'm sorry. I didn't."

She stopped to stare at him, took a deep breath, her fingers strumming against a glass countertop. "The vandals have struck again."

"Did you see anything?" Rick asked, concern for her safety overriding any other feelings and his own failings in not noticing.

"Oh, I saw enough."

"Did the alarm work?"

"Yes, the alarm did its job and the motion detector scared them away, thank goodness. The car took off in a hurry."

"But you saw the car?"

She nodded, pushed a hand through her hair. "A white convertible, top down." At his openmouthed surprise, she said, "The driver was wearing a dark hat. Hard to see who it was. But I think we both know who did this."

"Bridget," Rick said, shaking his head. "Are you sure?"

"I saw her car, Rick." Cari started gathering her stuff, then moved to turn off lights and lock doors. "Maybe I should just stay here and guard my property."

"What time did this happen?"

She shrugged. "Around ten-thirty or eleven, maybe."

Bridget had left the dinner at just past eight. Plenty of time for her to fume and go find a brick or two.

"Did the police come?"

"They came and listened to me rant and told me they can't do anything until I have solid proof."

"Did you tell them you thought it was Bridget?"

"Sure did. Even described the car. But they need a license plate number. Since I didn't get that, they can't do a whole lot and they suggested I shouldn't make unfounded accusations. So I'm stuck with having yet another repair to pay for." She sank down onto a round brocade stool. "I'm tired of this. I worked hard yesterday to get everything just right and now this. It's so silly, so ridiculous, even I find it hard to believe. A grown woman resorting to pranks to try and scare me away. She must really have it in for me, or she really has it bad for you." She grabbed her tote bag. "So how *was* dinner with Bridget last night, anyway?"

Rick could see the mad in her eyes, but he also saw a great sadness there, too. He grabbed her and halted her, his hands gentle on her arms. "You want the truth?"

She lifted her chin. "I'd like that, yes."

He stared down at her, wondering how she could infuriate him at the same time she endeared herself to him. "I was miserable at that banquet. Bridget finagled things so I would be at a table with Doreen and her."

"Oh, and I suppose you were just too polite to move to another table, right?"

"Well, yes." It sounded lame to his ears, too. "I got there late and dinner was being served, so I sat down and hoped I could get away."

"But you couldn't?"

This explanation wasn't going very well.

"No, not at first. Bridget wanted us to leave, but I told her no."

"That was thoughtful of you. What a sacrifice on your part."

"Look, Cari, I realized last night that I haven't handled things very well with Bridget. But I intend to do something about that."

"Oh, really. Better be careful. She might decide to slash your tires or something."

"That won't happen. Besides, I'm more concerned about what she might do to you. And that's the only reason I didn't talk to her about all of this last night."

"I can handle her," Cari retorted. "Because I've had enough. If I have to stay up all night long and get pictures, I'm going to prove that Bridget is behind this. I don't care how she feels, I'm not leaving town." Her gaze met his, determination in her bright eyes. "And I'm not going to quit seeing you either. That is, if you want to keep seeing me."

"I do want that," he said, glad she felt the same as he did. "That's why I'm going to have to be very clear with Bridget on where we stand."

Cari's expression softened but her tone was firm. "And I intend to do the same thing—tell both Doreen and Bridget how things stand."

Rick sat her down on the window seat. "Don't do anything crazy. I'm going to talk to Bridget and explain that I don't have any feelings other than friendship for her. I was wrong not to tell her that a long time ago."

"You think?" She got up and stomped around amidst the flash of glittery purses and flip-flops, her fingers touching on delicate brooches and earrings as she paced the now-full shop. "It's none of my business how you feel about Bridget or how she thinks she feels about you. But this, Rick, *this* is my business. And I just want to be left alone. I was on my way to talk to Doreen last night when you came by. But once I found out you'd probably be with both of them at dinner, I cooled my jets and decided I'd try to think positive. Well, that's over now. I'm going to sit them both down and explain that if they don't leave me alone I'll be forced to press charges. That is, if I can prove they're doing this."

This wasn't good. Not good at all. "How did you find out Bridget would be at the dinner?"

"Oh, she came by to get Brady and happened to *make sure* I knew you two had a 'date'."

"I'm so sorry. Why didn't you say something? I wouldn't have gone."

"It's not my place to tell you what to do."

No, she wouldn't be that way. Cari wasn't that kind of person. "I wouldn't have gone if I'd known," he repeated.

"No, I'm glad you went. Maybe now you can understand why I have to face them and get this over with."

Rick pulled her around. "Not right now. Right now, I want you to come with me to the ranch and relax. You're too keyed up to make a coherent decision about this. Give it some time and we'll figure out something together."

"I'm running out of time," she said. "They can't keep doing this after I open the shop."

Hoping to make her understand, he held her close. "Cari, are you hearing me? We'll find a way to clear things up. I don't care about Bridget, not the way I'm beginning to care about you. Do you understand what I'm trying to say?"

She looked up at him, her eyes full of doubt. "Do *you* even know what you're trying to say?"

"I think so. It's you, Cari. I care about you. That's all I understand."

"Then yes, you need to clue Bridget in on that. Because if she doesn't back off, I can't be responsible for my actions. I mean it, Rick. I've had it with her. It was bad enough when I lived with this as a teenager, but I was afraid to stand up to them then. I thought if I just took it, my father would defend me and believe me. But that didn't work. Now I have to do what I should have done back then— face them. The only reason I didn't go out to their house last night is because the police warned me to stay away until I had proof. I stayed up half the night trying to figure out how to get proof. But I will confront both of them. I mean it."

Rick believed her. She wasn't the kind to just sit back and take this. Or at least she wasn't that way now. Maybe once, but not now. And that was the scary part.

"Fair enough," he said. "But only after you've cooled off and we can think this through, together. Promise me that?"

She looked down then lifted her head again. "I can't promise you anything. This is something I have to do. It's the only way I can stay here. I have to show them that I'm not a threat to them. No matter what they think about me. And I need to show them that I've changed. I won't be pushed out of my own home again."

At least that statement sounded better than rushing in with bitterness and resentment. "Okay," he said, pulling her into his arms. "I told you, you're not alone anymore. And I've learned a hard lesson dealing with Bridget. I'll stop flirting with her and make sure she understands that I was only trying to be a friend to her. Nothing else. But I won't even attempt that anymore. I'll make it clear to her that she has the wrong impression regarding my feelings for her." Touching his lips to Cari's ear, he whispered, "And I'll show you that my feelings for you are very real."

Cari didn't say anything, but she did relax into his arms. Rick held her there for a long time then helped her lock up and set the alarm. But by the time he'd driven them out to the ranch, she'd settled down into a quiet resolve that worried him more than her anger ever could.

Cari watched as Rick threw a stick so his dog Shiloh could run and fetch it. The dog was adorable, all golden and furry and friendly. And the ranch was beautiful.

Rick had given her the guided tour an hour

earlier. The main house was a big, sprawling log-cabin style with a wraparound porch that made it look welcoming and cozy. The furnishings inside were country and quaint but not too chintzy since Rick shared the space with his brother when he didn't have to stay in town in the apartment over the store. His mother had opted to move to a smaller cabin around the bend after their father passed away. It was located near the big cabin but gave each of them their privacy.

And apparently, his brother Simon craved his privacy.

"He stays in his workshop out back day and night," Rick explained. "He was always introverted but since his wife died, well, the man has become more of a hermit than ever. I wish he could find someone to bring him back to life."

Cari's heart hurt for Simon Adams. He'd been deeply in love with his beautiful wife, but cancer had taken her at an early age. Since Cari could relate to that kind of grief after losing her parents, she felt an instant bond with Simon. Even if he did scowl and grunt a lot.

Now Rick ran back up the bank toward her then fell onto the old wooden bench. Below them the Chattahoochee gurgled and flowed, its swift current moving all the way through Georgia to join up with the Flint River and then eventually flow into the Apalachicola River in Florida and the Gulf of Mexico. He'd been right about bringing her here. She felt calmer now, her head clear.

"I love your place," she said, hoping he'd forget her earlier temperamental outburst—hissy fit number four. "Thanks for bringing me here."

He glanced behind them where his horse Pepper grazed with the mare she'd been riding. "I'm glad you came."

"Do you bring all of your girlfriends out here?"

She watched as his expression became wary. "Uh, who wants to know?"

Seeing the amusement in his eyes, she pushed at his arm. "It's a fair question. Answer it."

He laughed then looked out over the river. "You're the first, Princess."

Cari was touched but stunned. "You're serious? You've never brought another woman out here? Not even Bridget?"

He looked at his watch. "Two hours. Pretty good."

"What do you mean by that?"

"I mean her name didn't come up between us for two whole hours."

"Very funny." But she needed to know. "Has she been here?"

"No," he said, taking her hand in his. "She's asked to come, but it just didn't seem right." He shrugged. "This place is special. Simon works here, so he doesn't like gawkers and Mom likes her privacy after dealing with people all day long at the store."

"Then maybe I shouldn't be here."

"No, hear me out. That's not the problem. The thing is—we have this unwritten pact that we only bring special people up to the ranch. It's our getaway. Mom and I work hard at the store all week, so we try to get out here on the weekends at least."

"But you don't always stay out here."

"No. We have an apartment over the store. It's been there since the original owners lived there. We keep it so we can rest on our lunch breaks and I have an office up there. So sometimes Mom or I stay in town."

She grinned. "So I can rest safely some nights knowing you're nearby."

"Yes, ma'am, you certainly can." He pulled her into his arms. "And I'll rest better staying there until you get this vandalism stuff cleared up."

Cari settled her head against his shoulder. "You don't have to do that. I have the alarm now."

"I don't mind. Besides, next week will be crazy with tourists and shoppers. I'll be too beat to drive up here."

Cari thought about the upcoming week. "I'll do a dry run from Monday till Thursday. Then we'll have the grand opening right before the Fourth. That gives us the whole weekend to bring in customers. This will be my first test."

"You're gonna do fine," he said, kissing the top of her head. "It's a great location and you've brought something different and unique to the downtown area. Can't miss."

"I hope you're right." She turned to look up at him. "And I hope whoever is trying to torment me will leave me alone during the holiday weekend. Maybe Bridget will go out of town or something."

"Let's hope so." Then he lifted her chin. "But for now, let's talk about something else."

"Such as?"

"This," he said, lowering his head toward hers.

Cari accepted his kiss with open arms, her joy pushing aside her worries. After the kiss, she lifted her head. "I love the way you change the subject."

He nuzzled her cheek. "I'm good at what I do."

She kissed him again. "You certainly are."

They sat there watching the sun set over the river and the trees, the scent of mountain laurel and his mother's fat, lush daylilies filling the gloaming. Cari wished she could stay right here forever but that was impossible. She'd just have to cherish this sweet memory when the going got tough.

And she had no doubts that this next week would either make or break her chances of being successful in Knotwood Mountain. And possibly successful in loving Rick, too.

Chapter Seventeen

Cari heard the noise even before the flood-lights came on. Looking at the clock, she got up and threw on a robe over her cotton pajamas. It was three in the morning and someone was prowling around down on the porch.

Hurrying through the dark house, she wondered what they'd try this time. Would they tear down the red, white and blue bunting she'd so carefully strung across the newly painted porch railings for tomorrow's Independence Day celebration? Would they try to break into her shop and destroy her precious things? Or would they leave another ugly message to scare her?

"Not this time," she said, her flashlight in one hand and a baseball bat in the other. She wouldn't do bodily harm unless she came face-to-face with someone. But she wanted to be armed just in case.

Checking the alarm box by the kitchen door, she breathed a sigh of relief to see the green light blinking. So far, so good. Maybe the prowler had run away this time.

Then she heard Shiloh's distinctive bark from next door. Rick had brought the dog into town to help Cari protect her property. And sure enough, Shiloh was barking away in the upstairs apartment over the general store.

"Good dog," Cari whispered as she tiptoed down into the shop, careful to stay back in the shadows so she could watch through the big bay windows.

And she saw a shadow hovering there under the lights.

A brave soul, since the yellow glow from the security lights had to be centered on the entire porch and small front yard.

Stepping closer, Cari watched as the figure crept along the wall of the house. Then she saw a hand going up to the wall. The culprit was painting something on her pretty pale yellow house!

"That's it," Cari said, stomping toward the

front door. She didn't care if the alarm went off and woke the whole town. She intended to catch this person once and for all.

Yanking open the door, Cari rushed out with the baseball bat held high. Looking down the long porch, she saw the figure stepping backward toward the side railing. "Stop right there. The cops are on the way."

The alarm sounded in the still night. Maybe the police would listen to her now at least. But the shadowy figure, all dressed in black, dropped the can of spray paint and turned and hopped over the porch railing.

Cari ran down the steps and screamed, "Stop, you coward. I mean it. I'm going to press charges."

Rushing around to the alley, she watched as a white convertible cranked and gunned it down the street beside the house, its tires peeling rubber.

"Bridget." She knew it now because she had a partial plate number, one that would be hard to forget. She'd caught a glimpse from the streetlights. But it would be enough. It began with the letters *B-R-I*. And it didn't take much to fill in the rest. Bridget had a vanity plate with her name on it.

"Cari?"

She turned to find Rick and Shiloh running toward her. The dog was barking in a loud candence while the alarm shrilled over and over. "Let me turn off the alarm," she shouted. "I'm okay."

They followed her back to the front and she rushed inside to key in the code. Rick calmed down Shiloh and then the night went silent and still.

But Cari saw the lights from a patrol car outside.

"I saw her this time, Rick," she said. "It was Bridget."

He looked as disgusted as she felt. "You're sure?"

"I saw the car and got a partial plate number, but no, I didn't see her face. She was wearing that black hoodie again. She had a can of spray paint."

Cari hurried to the front porch, her flashlight in her hand. Nodding to the two officers coming up the steps, she said, "The vandal struck again and I got a partial plate. It was Bridget Stillman."

Then she flashed the light up against the wall to find something written in black: "Closed for Business. Permanently."

"Somebody's trying to shut you down,

Ms. Duncan," one of the officers said, shaking his head. "And you're sure it was the Stillman girl?"

"I'm sure it was her car," Cari replied, doubt rearing inside her. She had to be completely sure. She told them about the license plate.

"We'll run it through," the other officer said. "I'll go do that while you give your statement. Then we'll see what happens."

Cari nodded then told the other officer what had happened while Rick stood looking on, his hair tousled, his old T-shirt and gym shorts rumpled.

"Thank you," she said, smiling over at him. Then she reached down to pet Shiloh. "And thank you, too."

She'd just finished her statement when the other officer came rushing back in the open door. "The plates match Bridget Stillman's vehicle, but we've got other problems now."

"What?" Cari asked, surprised at the shocked look on the man's face.

"That vehicle was just in a one-car accident out on the South River road. Ran into a tree. I heard it over the radio. I gotta go."

"Oh, no." Cari turned to grab Rick. "We

have to go out there. She might be hurt. Rick?"

"Get dressed," he said. "I'll bring the Jeep around."

She couldn't stop shivering. Cari watched as the paramedics went back into the water where the convertible was partially submerged. They'd had to get the Jaws of Life to bring the unconscious driver out of the mangled vehicle.

And no one would tell her if the driver was Bridget and if the person was dead or alive.

"Rick," she whispered, holding to his shirt. "This is all my fault."

He pulled her into his arms. "You can't say that. You were trying to protect your property. You didn't force her to drive too fast for this curve."

"But I did force the issue. I should have talked to her, asked her to stop."

"It's okay," he replied. Then he shook his head. "I had a talk with Bridget this morning—about everything. I told her the truth—that I had feelings for you. She didn't take it very well. So if this is anyone's fault, it's mine."

Cari put a hand to her mouth. "Surely she

wouldn't do anything crazy just because you rejected her."

Rick looked down. "I hope not. Let's pray that she's going to make it."

But Cari knew if something happened to Bridget, it wouldn't be okay. And no matter what Rick had said to Bridget, it *would* be Cari's fault. How could it have come to this? She closed her eyes and prayed over and over for God to help Bridget. She didn't dare ask Him to forgive her. She just wanted Bridget to be alive.

Rick touched her shoulder. "Cari, they're bringing her out."

Cari rushed forward, calling to one of the officers. "Is it Bridget Stillman?"

He turned around to stare at her then shook his head. "No, ma'am."

"What?" Rick stepped forward. "Then who was driving that car?"

The officer's expression looked grave. "Her brother—Brady Stillman. He was behind the wheel. We ID'd him from his driver's permit."

"Brady!" Cari pushed past the officer. "Brady?" She rushed to the gurney, trying to see him. "Is he all right?"

Rick tugged her back, but she kept shouting. "Somebody tell me if he's alive?"

One of the paramedics nodded. "He's alive but he's unconscious. We've got him stabilized. It doesn't look good."

Then Cari saw him. He was wearing a black hoodie, drenched now and torn away from his body by the people who'd worked to save his life. "Brady," she whispered, her hand at her mouth. "Oh, dear God, please let him live."

As the EMT workers lifted him into the ambulance, she turned to the officer standing by her. "Have you called his mother?"

"She's going to meet us at the hospital."

Cari reached for Rick. "I have to go."

"Okay." He guided her toward the Jeep. When he had her safely inside, he stared down at her. "Cari, you understand what this means, don't you?"

Cari numbly bobbed her head, too shocked to do anything more. "Yes. It wasn't Bridget. It was Brady. He's the one who's been vandalizing me. And for the life of me, Rick, I can't understand that." She let out a little sob. "And right now, I don't care. I just want him to be okay."

Dawn poured over the courtyard by the waiting room, the sun's early rays pink and muted as they hit the bubbling fountain just outside the big windows.

Cari glanced over at where Doreen and Bridget sat stiff-backed, their worried expressions colored with fatigue. She'd only spoken to them briefly when they'd rushed into the hospital hours ago.

Doreen had looked at her in surprise. "What are you doing here?"

"I heard about the accident. I had to come."

And no one had questioned her further. They were all too worried about Brady. He was in surgery. Cari tried to remember what the doctors had told Doreen. A ruptured spleen, a collapsed lung, numerous abrasions and contusions. She couldn't remember the technical details. She just knew she wanted Brady to be fixed. She wanted everything to be fixed.

"How did you find out?" Doreen said now, breaking the taut silence surrounding them.

Cari looked up and into Doreen's questioning eyes. Now wasn't the time to tell her the truth.

"Yes, how did you find out?" Bridget's anger hit Cari in the face. Her gaze burned with hostility. "And why are you still here?"

Rick sat up, ready to come to Cari's

defense, but she put a hand on his arm. "I care about Brady. You both need to know that."

"We don't need you here," Bridget retorted. "You're not a part of our family anymore."

Her words hurt as badly as a slap in the face, but Cari swallowed her pain. "I understand that, but Brady and I…we were always close. And I saw him a few days ago. He helped me get things ready to open the shop."

"You were trying to turn him against us," Doreen said, the flare of hatred in her eyes overwhelming Cari.

"No, I'd never do that. I wouldn't." She looked over at Rick, saw the reassuring nod he gave her. "I just wanted to be a friend to him."

"He didn't need you," Doreen said, her designer purse held against her stomach like a shield. "You should have stayed away."

One of the officers who'd come to Cari's house walked up the hallway then sat down beside Bridget. "Sorry, Mrs. Duncan, but I have to ask some questions regarding the accident. I won't take long."

Doreen nodded, her focus still centered on Cari. "Make it quick. My head is splitting and I want to make sure I'm available when he comes out of surgery."

The officer nodded. "Why was Brady driving your car tonight, Miss Stillman?"

Bridget frowned over at him. "How would I know? I was on a date when my mom called. He must have sneaked it out of the garage."

"Did you give him permission to take the car, Mrs. Duncan?"

"No," Doreen said. "He was on restriction, so he wasn't allowed to drive even with me in the car. Like my daughter said, he took it without my knowledge."

"And why would he have been seen prowling around Miss Duncan's house on First Street?"

At that question, both Doreen and Bridget looked over at Cari, their expressions blazing with anger and shock.

"What on earth are you talking about?" Doreen asked. Before the officer could answer, she pointed at Cari. "What have you done? What was he doing at your house?"

Cari couldn't speak but Rick held up a hand. "I can explain that, Doreen."

And he told her about the attacks—the painted message on the parlor wall and the porch, the rocks through the turret room windows and the brick thrown into the sign on the front porch.

"We think he was behind all of this. Only we didn't realize it until tonight when Cari caught someone spray painting on her front porch."

Cari sat up, her hands open, palms up. "I saw the car and I thought it was Bridget. I was talking to the police when the call about the accident came over the police radio. I'm so sorry, Doreen. I had no idea."

Doreen stood up, her purse crashing to the floor. "You're sorry? Sorry? You scared my little boy so badly that he drove too fast and crashed his sister's car into a tree and went into the river? You're sorry!"

Rick stood between her and Cari. "Doreen, stop. This is not Cari's fault."

"No," Doreen said, anger making her spit out each word. "Nothing is ever Cari's fault, is it? The way her father changed after she broke his heart and left—that's not her fault, is it? Or me being in debt now because he was too sad and sick to run his business, I suppose that's not Cari's fault either?" She pointed toward Bridget. "Or the way my children were treated, ignored and verbally abused by her father because he was so upset about her, I guess that's not her fault at all. Because of her, he made our lives miserable. Miserable, do you hear? But that's not Cari's fault. Nothing is ever Cari's fault."

She stopped, tears running down her face. "You thought you were the one suffering all these years, didn't you? Well, you have no idea. No idea at all. Your father never loved me or my children the way he loved your mother and you. You won, Cari. You never knew that, but you won. He never got over losing your mother or you. And he made sure I knew that each and every day. And now my son who tried to reach out to you, to make you see, is in there close to death and you're telling me you're sorry, but you think he was trying to mess with you! How dare you!"

Cari sank down in her chair, sobs roiling like a giant undercurrent throughout her body. "Doreen, I had no idea. I never knew."

"Of course you never knew," Doreen shouted. "You never bothered to find out, did you? You never even tried."

Her rage spent, she fell into her chair then broke down, sobbing in Bridget's arms.

"Rick, I think you'd better get her out of here," Bridget said. "And to think I actually wanted you to notice *me*. You two deserve each other." Then she turned to the bewildered officer. "Is that enough of a statement for you?"

Without a word, Rick lifted Cari up and guided her toward the doors to the parking lot and into the Jeep.

Cari sat huddled as he drove through the quiet early-morning streets, her tears silent now as she thought back over everything that had happened since her father died.

Was Doreen right? Had Cari been so blinded by her own pain and grief that she'd failed to see her father's? That she'd failed to try and forgive him? Had he truly treated Doreen so terribly and become so miserable that everything he'd worked so hard for was now gone?

When Rick pulled the Jeep into the alley, he turned to her. "Cari?"

"I'm going in now," she said. "I can't talk about it right now, Rick. I need some time alone."

He came around to help her out of the vehicle. "I'm sorry," he said, his hands running through her hair. "I'm really sorry."

"So am I," she replied, pulling away toward the porch. She didn't look back but she knew this would probably be the last time she saw him. Because she was going inside to pack. She couldn't stay here.

"Cari, don't go," he said. When she didn't turn around, he bounded up the steps and forced her to stop at the door. "You can't run away. You were the one who said you had to face them. And you have. If you leave now, you won't be able to come back again."

"I don't intend to come back again."

Now Rick was the angry one. "And just like that, because you've finally seen the truth, you'll leave everything you have here."

"I don't have anything here."

The minute she said it, she regretted it. And she regretted the horrible hurt she saw in his beautiful eyes.

"Rick—"

"No." He backed away, his head down. "If you can't see what we have together, then you're right. You should go and you should stay away." He pivoted on the bottom step. "Because I can't live with you right next door, knowing that I love you and you can't love me in return. That would never work."

And with that, he walked away, back to his world.

And out of Cari's life.

* * *

Cari woke up from a troubled sleep to find it dark outside. And fireworks blasting through the night sky.

The Fourth of July celebration was underway.

But she didn't have a thing to celebrate.

She'd packed some clothes then fell down on her bed and cried her eyes out, finally falling asleep around dusk.

Today was supposed to be her grand opening.

Today was supposed to be the start of her new life here with Rick.

Now it was all over.

Getting up to wash her face, she looked at her cell phone. She'd turned it off, but now she flipped it open and watched it light up. Six messages from Jolena. None from Rick.

After getting a drink of water, she called Jolena.

"You're all right. Thank goodness."

Cari explained what had happened, her throat raw with pain.

"Honey, I know all of that and more," Jolena said. "I'm standing here outside the diner watching the fireworks. Come on out and I'll tell you what I heard."

"I can't," Cari said. "I'll just watch from the turret room, the way I did when I was little."

"Baby, you're gonna be okay," Jolena said. "Brady's gonna make it. He got through surgery and he woke up about an hour ago. Honey, he confessed to the vandalism. He's been asking for you."

Cari thought she couldn't cry anymore. She was wrong. "But why? Why Brady?"

Jolena's voice echoed over the line. "I'll come up and explain."

"Okay. I'll be in the turret room, but I'll unlock the back door for you."

Cari put down the phone and got dressed. She'd get up early tomorrow and go to see Brady. Then she'd leave before she had to face anyone else. But she at least owed Jolena an explanation.

So she sat down on one of the floral cushions she and Jolena had made for the window seat and watched the brilliant sparkling colors shooting through the sky, her heart remembering all she loved about this country and her town, even if that heart was broken. *How can I heal, Lord?*

When she heard footsteps on the stairs, she called out, "Up here, Jolena."

But when she turned to the door, Jolena wasn't standing there.

Rick stood there with a box in one hand and a burning sparkler in the other. "You're missing the show," he said. "So I brought part of it to you."

Tears pricked at Cari's eyes. The lone sparkler spurted in a pure electric white, its brilliance lighting up the whole room. She couldn't speak, couldn't move. Seeing him again hurt her so much, she thought her heart would shatter into pieces right there on the floor.

"What are you doing here?" she asked. "Jolena—"

"Sent me," he replied. "She didn't want to miss the grand finale."

"And what about you? Aren't you missing the highlight of the show?"

"Nope," he said as he watched the sparkler burn out then carefully put the now-blackened stick on the windowsill. "I don't like grand finales. They're just too *final*."

He put the box down then sat beside her. "I like grand openings, however. They're so…promising. But you missed yours."

"I won't be having a grand opening."

"Yes, you will." He tugged her close.

"Because I'm here to see that you don't go anywhere. Understand me? I'm here, Cari. Right here."

She saw the need and the sincerity in his eyes. "But Rick, look what I did. I turned my back on my father because of pride and bitterness. I could have helped him, but I didn't. If I'd only tried, things might be so different now."

"But you did try to make amends when he was dying. And you can do the same thing now, by staying."

"I don't know how to begin."

He kissed her cheek. "Running away won't solve that problem." He touched a hand to her hair. "When we turn from God, He waits for us. And all we have to do is turn around and accept His love and grace. You need to do the same now. You need to accept that I love you and I'm willing to fight for you. But not if you run from me."

"I wasn't running from *you*. I've just made such a mess of things. I didn't think I deserved you."

"I told you, this wasn't your fault. Brady was trying to scare you away so his mom could have this property. He thought he could help her get out of debt, thinking she could buy this cheap from you and then resell it to the highest bidder. Twisted logic, but then he loves her in spite of her flaws. And he heard her telling Bridget about how she'd like to flip the property and make a lot of money to help with the bills."

"But why did he help us with the renovations?"

"The kid was torn between helping you and helping his mom. And his friend Jeff knew about the vandalism, even helped him with some of it. He was holding it over Brady's head and pressuring him to keep doing it. Brady was caught between a rock and a hard place and things got out of hand. But none of that is your fault. You just got caught up in something that was already out of control."

Cari couldn't quite accept that. "So you love me in spite of my flaws?"

"I do." He kissed her lips. "I do. And if you stay, I'll spend the rest of my life trying to show you just how much."

Cari fell into his arms, her tears filled with joy now. He loved her. God loved her. And this time, she wanted to turn toward that saving grace instead of running from it.

She lifted up, her hands around his shoulders. "I love you, too, Rick. And I never want to disappoint you again."

"That won't happen." He kissed her then held her close. "We're gonna work this out, Cari."

She'd have to learn to trust him on that. "What's in the box?"

He grinned then pulled the wrapped box around. "Open it and see."

Cari tore through the bright paper and let out a gasp as she lifted the lid. "My red shoes."

"Your red shoes. I told you I'd save them for a special day." Then he took one out and lifted her foot, knocking her purple fuzzy slippers off. "I think you need to wear these on our wedding day." Placing the other one on her other foot, he said, "That is, if you'll marry me."

"Of course I will, after I take care of a few things." Cari looked down at her feet as the fireworks went into overdrive, blasting away outside the windows of her tiny turret room. "But I'd marry you without the shoes, you know."

"I brought them for leverage, just in case. And besides, Jolena strongly urged me to do it."

"Smart woman, Jolena." Then she touched

a hand to his face. "I'll have a long talk with Doreen and make my peace with her and Bridget, and I won't press charges against Brady." She took his hands in hers. "Will you take me to see him?"

He nodded, stroked her hair. "That's a good idea. Time for everyone to heal."

"Yes, time for everyone to heal." She'd make sure of that.

He nuzzled her neck then together they watched the last of the fireworks finale. The night sky lit up with brilliant yellows, reds, blues, whites and greens. Down on the crowded street, cheers went up.

Rick held her tight. "And tomorrow, bright and early, you are going to open your shop. We've already painted over the spot on the porch and your sign is back up. All you have to do is open the doors and let us in."

Cari turned in his arms, her sigh full of contentment. "It took me a while to figure that out, but I'm ready now."

Rick laughed and kissed her, the reflection of happiness from the celebration down on the street centered in his eyes. "Welcome home, Princess."

* * * * *

Dear Reader,

I love Cinderella stories but this one was a bit different. My modern-day Cinderella had been banished from her father's love because of a disagreement and because of the new woman in his life. Sometimes it's hard to accept change, especially when it comes so quickly on the heels of tremendous grief. But Cari Duncan had to do just that when her father remarried shortly after her mother's death. When Rick Adams heard Cari's story, he could tell she was filled with a bitterness that would never allow her to heal. Rick set out to show Cari that with God in her life, she is never alone.

I hope this story shows you that God is indeed there in every decision we make. Sometimes, in spite of knowing He's there, we still falter and make bad choices. But with God's grace and forgiveness, we can overcome grief and pain and heartache. God's love is always clear and He won't turn His back on us. While this story was a challenge, I worked at it until I got it right. It was a story that took control of my heart, so I hope you enjoyed reading it. There is a bit of Cinderella in all of us, I believe. We all want our Father's love. And God is ready and willing to give us that love.

Until next time, may the angels watch over you. Always.

Lenora Worth

QUESTIONS FOR DISCUSSION

1. Why did Cari come home to Knotwood Mountain? Was she out for revenge?

2. Why didn't Rick recognize her? Do you think it was about more than just her physical changes?

3. Did her father do the wrong thing in marrying so soon after her mother's death?

4. How would you handle a situation such as Cari's? Could you deal with a new person taking over your life?

5. Jolena was Cari's godmother. How did she help change Cari for the better?

6. Do you have someone like Jolena in your life? A person who offers you wise counsel?

7. What promise did Cari make to her parents when she went to visit their graves?

8. Why did Cari love Duncan House so much? Do you have a special place you remember?

9. Why did Brady try to scare Cari away? Why did he bother to help her even when he wanted her gone?

10. Do you think Cari was wrong to blame Doreen and Bridget for her troubles?

11. Do you think Doreen's life with Cari's father was a fairy tale?

12. How did Cari come to terms with the changes in her life? How did Rick help her?

13. Do you believe that Cari can forgive Doreen after learning the truth—that Doreen suffered as much as Cari did?

14. Do you think a person can go home again and start over?

15. Why were the red shoes so important as a symbol to Cari? Do you think she realized it wasn't about the shoes after all?

Here's a sneak preview of
THE RANCHER'S PROMISE
by Jillian Hart
Available in June 2010
from Love Inspired

"So, are you back to stay?" Justin's deep voice hid any shades of emotion. Was he fishing for information or was he finally about to say "I told you so"?

"I'll probably go back to teaching in Dallas, but things could change. I'll just have to wait and see." The things in life she used to think were so important no longer mattered. Standing on her own two feet, building a life for herself, healing her wounds—that did.

"And this man you married?" he asked. "Did he leave you or did you leave him?"

"He threw me out." She waited for Justin's reaction. Surely a man with that severe a frown on his face was about to take delight in the irony. She'd turned down Justin's love, and her husband of five years had thrown away hers. If she were Justin, she would want her off his land.

"You were nothing but honest with me back then." He leaned against the railing, the wind raking his dark hair, and a different emotion passed across his hard countenance. "I was the one who never listened. I loved you so much, I don't think I could hear anything but what I wanted."

"I loved you, too. I wish I could have been different for you." Helpless, she took another step toward the driveway. She didn't know how to thank him. He could be treating her a lot worse right now, and she would deserve it. "Goodbye, Justin."

"I suppose you need a job?"

"I'll figure out something." Need a job? No, she was frantic for one. How did she tell him the truth?

Find out in
THE RANCHER'S PROMISE
Available June 2010
from Love Inspired